The Open Window

by

Glen Ebisch

The Open Window

Cover Art by *Kim Mendoza*

The Wild Rose Press, Inc.
PO Box 708
Adams Basin, NY 14410-0708
Visit us at www.thewildrosepress.com

Publishing History
First Mainstream Mystery Edition, 2017
Print ISBN 978-1-5092-1601-7
Digital ISBN 978-1-5092-1602-4

Published in the United States of America

"Professor Teller is dead,"

he announced in the low controlled voice he used when upset.

Teller had been his journalism instructor when he was an undergraduate at Minton State University here in Minton, Massachusetts. He had been Daniel's mentor and the determining influence that had sent him on to a career in journalism. Daniel had majored in English with a minor in journalism, graduating from Minton State five years ahead of me. I'd majored in criminal justice with a minor in English. I'd figured it would help me with those police reports.

"I'm sorry. I know you were close. What did he die of?"

"He fell from his office window."

"Fell?" In my experience as a cop, people rarely fell from windows. Usually, there was some intentionality involved, like a helpful shove.

Daniel gave a sarcastic laugh. "Yeah, that's the question, isn't it? Did he fall, jump, or get pushed?"

"Sometimes an accident is just an accident," I said doubtfully.

"Teller wasn't disabled or senile. He'd been in that office for decades. What are the odds that he fell?"

"What are the odds that he jumped? Didn't you tell me his wife had just died a year or so ago? Maybe he was depressed."

"I talked to him within the last two weeks, and he didn't sound despondent."

"Sorrow is the sort of thing that can come in waves."

Daniel grunted his disbelief.

Praise for Glen Ebisch

Mr. Ebisch has had over twenty-five books published, mostly mysteries. His last book, *STORMY WEATHER*, was published by The Wild Rose Press, Inc. Some of his previously published books have been reviewed in Publishers Weekly and The Kirkus Review.

Chapter One

The Hastings were going at it again. So what else was new? We were in the kitchen, which the previous owners had recently redone. As usual, what the husband liked, the wife hated, and vice versa.

"This is a complete gut job," Marcie Hastings announced, waving her hand as if it were a magic wand that would make the beautiful cherry wood cabinets and dark granite countertops disappear. "I want white cabinetry and light counters. This is just gloomy. I'd get depressed cooking supper."

"When was the last time you cooked supper?" her husband Roger mumbled, just loud enough to be heard.

She shot him a venomous glance but didn't respond.

"This kitchen is beautiful. It would be criminal to change it—*criminal*," Roger said, his voice rising to a crescendo.

"You want to leave this, but replace that marvelous chandelier in the front entry?" his wife asked.

"That looks like it belongs in a bordello."

"What would you know about that?" she asked suspiciously.

"You're driving me to it," he muttered so that only I could hear.

"What was that?" his wife said.

"Nothing."

I urged them on into the family room and put my hearing on hold. I pretty much knew what they would say based on the ten houses I had already shown them. Fixing in place my polite, patient realtor's face, I let the sounds wash over me while the Battle of Hastings, as I liked to think of it, recalling my one British history course, unfolded.

There is nothing like house hunting to bring out the fault lines in a marriage, and I suspected the Hastings' marriage had fissures rivaling the San Andreas Fault before they ever decided to search for a new home and by some stroke of misfortune ended up at my desk. I'd only been doing this job for two years, but even in that relatively brief time, I'd come to realize that you had to let the couple fight it out. Getting caught in between as a mediator never helped to make a sale. It was a war of attrition, and either they would end up exhausted and stay where they were, or they would eventually realize that compromise was essential to accomplish a move. I wasn't sure, as of yet, which way the Hastings were going to go.

Twenty minutes later, after proceeding through serial disagreements in every room of the house, we were out in the driveway again. Although glaring at each other, they both managed to muster grudging smiles and thank me for showing them the home, which they told me, as if I hadn't already realized it, was not exactly right for them. I smiled sadly and said I'd be in touch as soon as something I deemed appropriate appeared on the market. Then I waved to them with forced gaiety as they backed down to the road.

Ten minutes later, after I had turned out all the lights, locked the doors, and sighed a couple of times, I was standing next to my car admiring the beautiful fall weather of late September in New England when my phone rang. I pulled the phone out of my jacket pocket and saw that the call was from my boyfriend, Daniel Rencardi.

"Hi, Daniel, what's going on?"

"Professor Teller is dead," he announced in the low controlled voice he used when upset.

Teller had been his journalism instructor when he was an undergraduate at Minton State University here in Minton, Massachusetts. He had been Daniel's mentor and the determining influence that had sent him on to a career in journalism. Daniel had majored in English with a minor in journalism, graduating from Minton State five years ahead of me. I'd majored in criminal justice with a minor in English. I'd figured it would help me with those police reports.

"I'm sorry. I know you were close. What did he die of?"

"He fell from his office window."

"Fell?" In my experience as a cop, people rarely fell from windows. Usually, there was some intentionality involved, like a helpful shove.

Daniel gave a sarcastic laugh. "Yeah, that's the question, isn't it? Did he fall, jump, or get pushed?"

"Sometimes an accident is just an accident," I said doubtfully.

"Teller wasn't disabled or senile. He'd been in that office for decades. What are the odds that he fell?"

"What are the odds that he jumped? Didn't you tell me his wife had just died a year or so ago? Maybe he was depressed."

"I talked to him within the last two weeks, and he

didn't sound despondent."

"Sorrow is the sort of thing that can come in waves."

Daniel grunted his disbelief.

"When did this happen?"

"About twenty minutes ago. I got a call from Bianca. She's on the scene, but the police won't let her into the building."

Bianca Fitzsimmons had been the regular crime reporter—if you could call her that—for the past three months on *The Sentinel*, the newspaper Daniel published fours days a week. His staff was part-time, except for an office manager, and Bianca was actually a journalism student at Minton State. I'd never met her in person, but I wasn't surprised she couldn't get past the police at a crime scene; even a veteran reporter would have been stopped.

"I was hoping that you could go there and try to get in. Detective Harrington no doubt will be in charge, and he owes you. After all, you saved his wife's life when you were on the force."

It was my turn to grunt. I didn't like to trade on what I did during my time as a cop.

"I'm not a reporter, I'm a real estate agent. What would be my reason for wanting access to the crime scene?"

"How about I make you a reporter for this one story? You do some of the heavy investigating, and Bianca writes the copy."

"You know I've avoided being involved with the department since my retirement. This would throw me right into the middle of an ongoing police investigation."

Daniel cleared his throat. "I know, and I'm sorry to ask this of you, Kate, but Teller was important to me. I really want to find out how he died."

"The police will find that out. Harrington is a good man."

"I know he is, but the chief is ultimately in charge. We both know how you feel about him."

Chief Randal and I had a history, but that was just another reason for me to stay out of his way.

"He may not be much of a human being, but he's a competent cop," I replied.

"How about you just go over and take a look?" Daniel urged. "I'll let it go if it's clearly an accident or suicide. If there's anything dodgy, we'll talk about how to proceed."

I knew I was being manipulated. Daniel was good at it. I'd frequently watched him persuade others to do what he wanted. I was tempted to refuse, but there was a small creature in the back of my brain that was curious about what had happened. The same creature that had gotten me to join the force in the first place and that still wasn't completely satisfied with the role of Kate Cameron, Realtor.

"I'll go over and see if I can get in. But there's no guarantee Harrington will let a civilian on the scene."

"A reporter, there is a difference."

"Not necessarily for the better." I knew Daniel was getting ready to muster more arguments to convince me to see things his way, so I hurried on. "Don't worry, I'll give it the old college try. Where was this fatal window?"

"Dillard Hall. You know where it is? It's the oldest building around the quadrangle. I'll give Bianca a call and have her meet you there."

"How will we know each other?"

"What are you wearing?"

I described my tan slacks, yellow blouse, and navy blazer.

"Don't worry there won't be many women six feet tall with chestnut hair in their mid-twenties dressed for business hanging around outside Dillard Hall. She'll spot you. Bianca is a smart young woman."

"What does she look like?"

"About five-two, short dark hair, and bright eyes."

I wasn't sure I liked the sound of the description or that it came so easily to Daniel's lips.

"How about we get together tomorrow at eleven in *The Sentinel* offices to compare notes?" Daniel suggested. "Can you make that?"

"Sure."

"And Kate?"

"Yes."

"Thanks for doing this for me."

"No problem," I replied, not sure I was doing it for him or for myself.

Chapter Two

The campus of Minton State University is on the west side of Minton heading out toward the foothills of the Berkshires. It was part of the Massachusetts state system and had been only a college until the state in a swift policy shift had somehow managed to upgrade all the state institutions to university status a few years ago. Nobody in town complained. Since Minton was a small city of around sixty-five hundred, the college was a big part of its economy, and any upgrade, even one in name only, was appreciated.

I pulled into a parking lot assigned to visitors. I got out of the car and took a deep breath. The scent of the pine trees and the clear fall air made me a bit nostalgic for my student years. My time at Minton State had been good. I'd met lots of great people, and been looking forward with enthusiasm to a career on the police force. If I'd known then what I knew now, I might not have been so happy. Maybe I'd even have changed my major. But for better or worse the gears of life don't go in reverse.

I walked between the more recent buildings that made up the outer ring of the university. The quadrangle was the original center of the college, which had grown in concentric circles out from that core. I was surprised at how much had changed in the six years since I'd been a student there: new buildings and stylish landscaping gave the place a contemporary, well cared for look. Despite the changes, I easily found my way to the quadrangle. Dillard Hall wasn't hard to spot given the police officer on the steps and the student presence around the front door. It was a large fieldstone structure that looked to be from the late nineteenth century. It must have been sandblasted recently because it was lighter than the ones on either side of it.

I followed the path across the quadrangle and made my way through the crowd of students milling around in front of the building. No one ran up to me and identified herself as Bianca Fitzsimmons, so I proceeded up the steps to where a young cop was standing by the front door. I stayed one step below him to allow him his feeling of specialness. He was unfamiliar, probably a hire since I left the force. "Carson" was the name on his badge.

"This building is off-limits, ma'am," he said, looking over my head as if I wasn't there.

Since he couldn't have been more than a couple of years younger than me, the "ma'am" really rankled.

"Is Detective Harrington up there?" I asked.

His eyes drifted down in my direction but stayed at the level of my forehead. He didn't answer. Someone along the way had probably told him that not responding to the public made him look tough and professional. Actually, it made him look like a jerk.

"Would you get on your little microphone there," I said, pointing to the radio attached to his shirtfront, "and let Detective Harrington know that Kate Cameron is here and would like permission to come up?"

There was a flicker of recognition behind his eyes that told me he'd heard my name before. For better or worse, I was something of a legend on the force.

Moving with extra slowness as if to prove that no civilian was going to make him do anything with dispatch, he keyed in his radio and repeated my message. A minute later, permission came back. I smiled to myself at the thought that Harrington and I were still friends. I stepped up until I was on the level with Officer Carson. Now I was taller than he was, and Officer Carson didn't look pleased. I stared at him until he moved away from the door.

"Go up to the third floor and take a right," he said in a voice hoarse from disuse as I went past him.

I walked up the marble stairs sliding my hand along the wrought iron railing. They certainly didn't make buildings like this anymore. Solid and reliable, it felt like a place where learning would happen by osmosis. There were a couple of uniforms to my right down the hall on the third floor, so I headed in that direction.

I spotted Detective Jim Russell, who, along with Harrington, made up the entire detective unit. He gave me a neutral nod and pointed toward the half open door. I pushed the door open. It gave a hesitant squeak, enough to get Harrington to look over from across the room where he was talking with a state forensics specialist. After saying a few more words to the man, he walked across the room toward me.

"How are you, Kate?" he said with a warm smile, putting out his hand.

"Never better, Dennis, and you?"

He shrugged.

"And how's Amy?"

"The wife's fine. Are you still in the real estate

game?"

"If you ever want to sell that old colonial of yours, keep me in mind."

"I just may do that. It costs me five hundred dollars a month in winter to heat, and that's keeping the thermostat set to where my fingers turn blue. And don't get me started on the home repairs."

"I could sell your place and get you into a nice new condo where you'll never have to look at a hammer again and still have a bundle of money left over to put in the bank."

He raised his eyebrows. "Are you sure we're talking about my old dump?"

"It's a dump with a good location, and as you know, that's the name of the game."

"I'll give it some thought." His eyes wandered across the room to where the forensics team was beavering away in the shadowy corners. When his gaze came back to me it had hardened. "So what are you doing here, Kate?"

"Professor Teller was an old friend of Daniel's. He asked me to cover the story."

"I didn't know you worked the crime beat for *The Sentinel*. I thought it was that girl Bianca who was around here earlier."

"I guess Daniel wanted someone a little more seasoned to be involved in this one."

"And someone that I might talk to about the case?"

I smiled. "That was probably on his mind."

Harrington sighed. "You know there isn't a day goes by when I don't thank my lucky stars that you were coming out of that library door just when you were. Amy would be dead if you hadn't been there.

There's no way I can express my appreciation to you for what you did. But if the chief ever found out that I was involving you in an investigation, my life wouldn't be worth living."

"I'm not asking to be involved. Treat me like a reporter. Give me the facts, and I promise not to publish until you give me the go-ahead. Any investigating I do will be completely on my own, and I'll let you know anything I turn up."

Harrington nodded. "The Chief won't be happy just knowing I let you up here. And he will find out, he's got his spies everywhere."

"Just tell him you were keeping the press sweet. If he has any complaints, let him get in touch with Daniel."

"Okay, we'll try and see how it goes. But I may have to cut you off without warning."

"Understood. What do you have so far?"

"Apparently Professor Teller went out the window sometime around one-fifty. Nobody actually saw him fall, but two students found his body as they were on their way to class. This is a pretty busy pedestrian walkway, so if he had fallen earlier, he probably would have been spotted."

"Maybe. But the students are in class from one until around one-fifty, so during that time there might not have been much traffic within sight of the side of the building."

"Good point."

"So nobody saw anything. Did anyone hear anything?" I asked.

He shook his head. "We took a quick survey of the hall when we got here. There was one guy in his office down on the other side. He didn't hear anything. The folks in the English Department office are pretty far up the hall, and heard nothing."

I walked across the room, being careful not to touch anything, and stared at the window. "It's a very tall window, and there's no screen. It wouldn't be hard to accidentally fall out."

"Teller was over six three, so he could have lost his balance and toppled over the sill."

"Did he have any disabilities or balance problems?"

"We don't know yet. There was no cane or walker in the room." Harrington cleared his throat. "We're actually leaning toward suicide. The dean came rushing over here as soon as we arrived. He said that Teller's wife had died only a year ago, and he'd been distraught. Also, he was under some career pressures."

"What's the dean's name?"

"Messing, Carl Messing."

"Do you mind if I have a chat with him?"

Harrington nodded his head. "Just wait until tomorrow. We'll interview him today."

I walked closer to the window and looked down. The body was gone, but there was a large, dark stain on the walk going around the building.

"We're only on the third floor, not really that high up. If he had cleared the sidewalk and reached the lawn, he might have lived. It doesn't seem like a surefire way to commit suicide."

"I thought the same thing. But you know how suicides are; they get an idea into their heads and don't always reason it through. It might have been an impulse thing."

"Daniel had a talk with Teller recently, and he seemed pretty upbeat."

"Like I said, it could have been on impulse. Good one day; bad the next."

"One sure thing, no one crept in here and pushed him out the window. Not with that squeaky door. He'd have heard him coming," I said.

"Not necessarily. He was having an office hour, and he had the door open. We've checked. It was open when the security people got here to see what had happened. I suppose he could have been standing by the open window when someone slipped in and gave him a shove. It's a nice day. He might have had the window open to get some air. These old buildings can get pretty stuffy."

"I suppose no one has told you about him having any enemies out to kill him?"

Harrington smiled. "Not yet, but I plan to ask around."

I nodded and stretched out my back.

"How has your back been, Kate?

"Fine, just like it was three years ago when they put me on desk duty for the rest of my life."

"They shouldn't have done that. It was nothing but jealousy. But you showed them, applying for disability retirement and using their own lies against them. I guess they thought you would just quit."

"I'm not a quitter, Dennis."

"Anyone who knows you realizes that. Is there anything else I can help you with?"

"No. So you don't mind if I poke around in the case a little, as long as I don't get in the way?"

He sighed. "I suppose not. As long as you let me

know what you find."

"I'll stay in touch."

We shook hands again, and I made my way out of the building. Carson was still on the top step glaring at the crowd as if he were the thin blue line holding back a mob from swarming the building. I was making my way through the group of students when a short, perky young woman rushed up. She was cute and definitely bright-eyed.

"I'm Bianca Fitzsimmons," she announced, putting out a small hand that disappeared into mine. "Sorry I wasn't here to meet you. I had to go to my psychology class. The professor is a bear about attendance."

"Going to class is good," I said. "After all you are a student."

I immediately regretted sounding so stodgy and maternal.

"What I *actually* am is a reporter. Going to school is just a way to become that—full time."

"Okay," I said, smiling to suggest a cease-fire.

"Daniel is giving me my big chance."

I nodded. The way she said Daniel's name, almost with reverence, made me uneasy. I also wasn't sure how much of a break working for *The Sentinel* really was for a budding reporter.

"Yeah, Daniel is a nice guy."

"You're right." She gave me a searching look. "But of course you'd say that, you're his girlfriend."

I caught something in her tone suggesting that I wasn't deserving of that honor.

"Since we're going to be working on this story together, perhaps we should compare notes," I suggested.

"I'm the crime reporter for *The Sentinel*. You're a real estate agent."

I managed a smile at how she made my job sound vaguely disreputable. "But on this story we are working together, sharing a byline."

Her face went from cute to pouty. She was about to object.

"Daniel said so," I added, hoping the magical name would cut short any dispute.

"Okay, but I'm the regular reporter, so my name should come first."

"My last name is Cameron, yours is Fitzsimmons, mine should come first in alpha order."

Her attitude was clearly starting to rub off on me.

"Let's let Daniel decide," she said.

"Fine."

"If you're going to be a reporter on this story, what are you going to do next?" Bianca asked with a smooth smile as if I clearly would have no idea.

"I've already talked with the detective on the case. Tomorrow I plan to meet with Dean Messing."

"What are you going to talk to *him* about?" she asked, her face twisted in disgust.

"What have you got against the dean?"

"He's kind of a jerk. The students don't like him."

"Well, I thought maybe he could tell me something about Professor Teller's situation at the university."

"I think I can find out more by talking to students, particularly English majors."

"Why don't you do that then? And tomorrow we meet—

"At *The Sentinel* offices at eleven. I know, Daniel already told me."

"Great, see you then," I said with false cheerfulness and walked away before I said something I would regret.

I was a few yards away from the crowd when someone came running up behind me. I turned quickly at the sound of the footsteps. One of the things I'd learned on the job is that it's always better to confront things head on. A tall, thin, blond-haired guy who appeared to be a student skidded to a halt.

"Sorry to bother you," he said, blushing. "But I wondered if you're a police officer."

"No." I almost said that I was a realtor, then realized that would be confusingly off point, and said, "I'm a reporter."

"Oh, I thought you looked like someone official, being older and better dressed."

I smiled. "I'll take the second part of that as a compliment."

He blushed again, so I knew he got my point. "Sorry, I didn't mean to imply that you're old."

"Thanks for that. How can I help you?"

"I just wanted to know. Some students said that Professor Teller fell from his office window and is dead. Is that really true?"

"I'm afraid it is, and you are?"

"Evan Miller. I'm taking, or I was taking, an introductory journalism course with Professor Teller."

Setting my reporter's cap firmly in place, I decided it was time to ask a few background questions about the victim. I was sorry I didn't have one of those small spiral notebooks reporters always used to carry in the old days. Today they probably take notes on their cell phones.

"What did you think of Professor Teller?"

Evan paused. "He knew everything about journalism. You could ask him anything, and he'd have an answer based on his own experience."

"Was he an easy teacher?"

"No. He was pretty old school. There was a lot of reading and papers to write. And he could be kind of cranky if you asked what he thought was a stupid question."

"I didn't think any questions were stupid today."

"If it was something you should already have known from the reading, it was stupid."

"Got it. Did he seem to be a generally happy person?"

Evan shrugged. "Hard to tell. He didn't talk a lot about himself or show his emotions. Some of us who are English majors knew about his wife dying last year, but he never mentioned it. In class, he was all business." He looked over his shoulder, back at the building. "Do the police think he jumped?"

"I don't think the police have formulated a theory yet. They're still gathering information."

"Just like a good reporter does."

I smiled. "Is that what you want to be, a reporter?" Print journalism might be dead, but apparently not on this campus.

His face twisted. "No, that's way too gritty for me. I'm not a confrontational guy. I plan to be an English professor. I'm going on to graduate school next year."

"Good for you. Best of luck."

"Thanks. Well, I'd better be going," he said, with a toss of his blond head.

I nodded, and he turned and went off at a fast walk

toward the students still gathered in front of the building.

As I drove away from the campus, I mulled over Teller's death. Suicide was still the best call. Even though jumping from a window was an odd method to choose, Harrington was right, suicides frequently act on impulse. I found my mind drifting from the case to Bianca Fitzsimmons. I was still uneasy about the way she responded to Daniel's name. Even though he was more than a decade older than she was, youthful crushes are no respecters of age. I hoped Daniel knew what he was getting himself into.

Chapter Three

I had a closing to attend the next morning at ten. Since things had been a little slow lately and I hadn't sold a house in a couple of months, I was pleased to have this on the agenda. It was also nice because the buyers I represented were a young married couple that seemed very much in love. Although I'm not normally a gushy person, being involved in helping a new family start out in life did make me feel good. Realistically I knew they would have some bumps along the way, but they seemed like the kind of couple that could handle it.

Not all agents attend closings. However, I make a point of it because I feel it to be the last of my responsibilities to my clients, putting a finishing touch on the project, so to speak. Sometimes, like today, I'm happy to go and see them head on to the next stage of life. Other times, when the experience has been less pleasant, I just want to make sure that the deal finally goes through, so I won't have to work with the people again. On the whole, however, being a realtor shows you a better side of people than being a police officer, although I still find myself missing the force.

Since the lawyer's office where the closing was being held was only five blocks away from my office, and it was another beautiful fall day, I decided to walk. As I strolled along, I thought about the Teller case. I'd called the dean's office earlier that morning. Even after identifying myself as a reporter for *The Sentinel*, who was writing an in-depth piece on the life and work of Joseph Teller, the best I'd managed to do was get an appointment for tomorrow at eleven o'clock. I wondered what the career issues were that Dean Messing had alluded to in his conversation with Harrington. Since Teller was a full professor, he must have had tenure. Daniel had once told me, based on his experience in journalism school, that once you had tenure there was very little you had to worry about with regard to career security. So it seemed unlikely that professional concerns would have driven him to suicide. Considering the unlikelihood of his having fallen by accident, if suicide was also eliminated, that left only murder. I resisted the idea. True, people were murdered every day, occasionally it even happened in a city the size of Minton, but being shoved from a window would definitely be a rare event. As a cop, I'd learned that if you hear a four-legged animal with hooves racing down the road, it is far more likely to be a horse than a zebra. Expecting the unexpected only gets you into trouble and creates a lot more work— except when it's right and solves the case.

The closing went as smoothly as I had expected. Even Attorney Hascomb, whose family has been in Minton since Puritan times and who usually acts as if the practice of law is slow torture to him, came close to cracking a smile when the couple had spontaneously kissed upon receiving the keys to their new home. I left feeling a renewed confidence in humanity, and I'm sure my step was positively spritely, as I cut across the town green to *The Sentinel* offices, which are housed in a nineteenth century, two-story, brick office building.

Myra Kepler was sitting in her usual place behind the counter to my left as I entered. She had the phone to one ear and was writing on a yellow legal pad. She smiled and held up her index finger to indicate she'd be with me in a minute. Myra had the title of office manager, but in reality, she was the entire office staff and handled the classified listings as well as circulation complaints. Without her, the newspaper would fold. She was a member of the army of anonymous middle-aged women who keep the country functioning.

"How are you, Kate?" she asked while hanging up the phone and finishing her notes.

"I don't know yet. It depends on how this meeting goes."

"How did Daniel manage to rope you into doing this?"

I shrugged. "It seemed to mean a lot to him."

"He's always been close to Professor Teller, I guess. But even more so since his father died."

Daniel had left home after college and gone to the Columbia School of Journalism. After doing a lot of grunt work, he had managed to land a job as a reporter with a newspaper in Manhattan. When his father had died three years ago, he had returned home and taken over as managing editor of *The Sentinel.* Although he'd never complained about his decision in the short time we'd been together, I knew he had sacrificed a lot to be there for his mother.

"Yes. I guess Teller was really a mentor for him in college," I said.

Myra nodded toward the conference room door. "That's probably why he takes such an interest in *her.* He thinks of it as giving back."

"You mean Bianca?"

"There's a little miss who's not to be trusted. I'd keep an eye on her if I were you. If you ask me, she's as interested in Daniel as she is in being a reporter."

"Daniel has hardly mentioned her to me in the time she's been here." I wasn't sure whether that was a good thing or not. In a way, it was like hiding her in plain sight.

"Oh, don't get me wrong, I don't think Daniel has any interest in her. I doubt that he even realizes her intentions might be personal. For Daniel, it's all about the job. You know how men can be. They hardly notice how a woman feels about them until she hits them over the head."

"And you think Bianca is ready to do some hitting?"

"So far she's been pretty subtle, but you never know when she might decide to turn things up a few degrees. I think it's a good idea that you're involved in this story and can get some idea of what's going on."

"I'm sure there's nothing going on. I have absolute confidence in Daniel," I said, sounding a bit sniffy even to myself.

"I'm sure you do, but don't underestimate the appeal of a pretty young face." Myra stared down at her desk. "I made that mistake once. My first husband and his secretary, it hit me like a ton of bricks."

"I'm sorry."

"Water under the bridge, as they say, but you may as well learn from my experience. Pay attention to your man or somebody else will." Myra picked up the phone. "I'll let him know you're here."

She told him I was waiting and after a moment, the

door to the conference room opened and Daniel came out. I could see over his shoulder that Bianca was sitting at the table. Since I had arrived right on time, she must have come early in order to steal some alone time with Daniel. Myra was right; I'd have to keep an eye on her.

Daniel peered up at me over his reading glasses and smiled. He always looked so adorable with them on that I wanted to give him a big kiss. But I confined myself to a hug and a peck on the cheek. Daniel is only an inch taller than me, so I didn't have to stretch. His brown curly hair tickled my nose as I hugged him.

"How have you been?" I asked, standing back to get a good look at his face.

He gave me a crooked smile. "Pretty good under the circumstances."

"I'm very sorry about Professor Teller, I know he meant a lot to you."

"Yes. I think it's the suddenness of it all more than anything. I still feel like I'm in a state of shock." He stepped back and motioned for me to enter the conference room. "C'mon in. Bianca showed up a little early, so we've been talking about things."

I gave him a smile that I hoped stayed neutral. I walked into the conference room and said hello to Bianca. She gave me a little wave and sat there looking smug. I glanced around the room. I'd looked through the door a few times in the past, but never been inside. It had all the charm of the average police interrogation room: institutional green paint, a table of some generic material in the center, and no windows.

The owner of *The Sentinel* also published several other small papers in the western part of the state, and if these offices were any indication, he wasn't putting a lot of money into the operation. Daniel had told me that they just managed to get by on local advertising, so the last major redecoration of the offices had been during the peak of print journalism in the nineteen-fifties.

I took a seat on the opposite side of the table from Bianca. I had a feeling the positioning would be appropriate. Daniel settled into his chair at the head of the table. He took off his reading glasses and rubbed his face as if trying to erase his emotions.

"Detective Harrington gave us permission to write an obituary of Joe Teller," he began. "Since he had no children and his wife had died, we didn't have much personal information, and the funeral home couldn't help. But Bianca did some research on his professional life, and between us, we put together a good obituary that shows the significance of both his academic contributions and his earlier work as a journalist." He turned to the girl. "Thank you, Bianca."

She nodded earnestly, her eyes adoring, as if there were nothing she wouldn't do for him. I thought that just about captured the state of things.

"What did Harrington allow you to say about his death?" I asked.

Daniel cleared his throat. "We said it was the result of a fall. We weren't allowed to speculate on whether it was an accident or whether he jumped or was pushed."

I nodded. That sounded like the boundaries the police would place early on in an investigation.

"So what are we going to do next?" I asked.

"I was trying to come up with an approach that would allow us to stay involved in the investigation, so I suggested to Harrington that we might do a more in-depth retrospective on Teller's life: interview colleagues, talk to friends, that sort of thing. Maybe plan on getting it out in a week to ten days."

Bianca raised her hand like she was in class. "Would Kate and I be sharing the byline on that?"

"Do you have any objections?" Daniel asked her.

"None at all," Bianca replied sweetly. "But I think I should get first billing because I'm the regular crime reporter."

"Is that all right with you, Kate?" he asked.

"I thought it would be more appropriate in alphabetical order," I replied.

Daniel thought for a minute. "But Bianca does have a point."

"Of course she does," I replied, trying without complete success to keep the sarcasm out of my tone.

"So why don't we go with it that way, then," Daniel said, happy to have things resolved. "You both get credit, but Bianca's name goes first."

We both nodded. Bianca gave me a long look of triumph.

"So what point are we at in our investigations?" Daniel said, rubbing his hands together as if interested in getting down to the substance of things.

"The police are keeping an open mind as to the cause of death. If it was a suicide, the reasons might be the death of his wife or some career issues at the University," I said.

"His wife died almost a year ago. I'd be surprised if it was that," Daniel said. "What are these 'career issues'?"

"I don't know," I said. "Dean Messing is the one who mentioned them to the police. I have an appointment to meet with him tomorrow."

"Anything else?" Daniel asked me. I shook my head.

Bianca squirmed in her chair like she had *ants in her pants* as my Aunt Irma used to say. Finally, she couldn't control herself any longer.

"Well, *I've* found out that Dean Messing was pressuring Professor Teller to retire, so he could give his tenured position to Rockwell Brody, a male faculty member that he's having a romantic relationship with. He'd even taken away some of Professor Teller's writing courses and given them to Brody."

"How did you find all that out?" I asked after a shocked pause.

"By talking to a student, just like we agreed I would."

"What student in particular?"

A petulant look came over her face. "I promised the person they'd remain anonymous."

"Surely, you can tell us in confidentiality," Daniel said.

She shook her head. "If Kate knew who the person was, she'd want to go question that person."

Daniel glanced at me.

"I'd want to find out if Bianca's source was telling the truth," I admitted.

"And then before long, the cops would know their name, and it would get back to the University administration. The student could get expelled."

"What if I promised not to go see this person?" I asked.

Bianca shook her head. "It wouldn't matter. I promised confidentiality. You won't get the name out of me."

She raised her head with a brave look on her face as if determined to defy all the forces attacking her journalistic integrity, especially as personified by me. I looked behind her at the green wall and wished this were an interrogation room and I was still a cop. Then I'd get the name out of her.

"She does have a point," Daniel said to me. "Word might get back to the administration and jeopardize our source."

"This could be a murder investigation. Keeping secrets might be dangerous."

Daniel paused. "How about we compromise on this? Bianca can keep her secret for now, but if we develop some clear evidence that this is a murder case, then she has to reveal the name of her contact."

Reluctantly we both nodded.

"Fine," Daniel said, smiling steadily at our somber faces. He turned to me. "So you're going to interview Dean Messing tomorrow?"

"Yes. And I'd like permission to use the information Bianca has gathered about the dean in my questioning."

"That's my information," she objected. "I should be the one who gets to use it."

"Do you ever intend to graduate?" I snapped. "Because accusing your dean to his face of trying to remove a faculty member to get his lover a better job is probably a good way of guaranteeing that will never happen."

Bianca opened her mouth. Realizing the truth of my remark, she closed it again and sat there looking sullen.

"Don't worry," Daniel said to her in a reassuring voice. "I'll see that you get full credit for your fine piece of work."

Her face brightened, and she blushed at the compliment. She glanced at her watch.

"I'm afraid I have to go now. I have a class," she said, reaching over to pull her backpack off the chair next to her. She looked at Daniel and me, as if reluctant to leave us alone together.

"Don't worry," Daniel said, sensing her indecision, "the meeting is over."

"What would you like me to do next?" Bianca asked.

"Keep developing leads among the students. See if there could have been any other reason for Teller's death," Daniel suggested.

Bianca nodded eagerly and stood.

"Bye now," I said. She ignored me.

"Thanks for coming," Daniel said, standing politely.

"You're welcome." She leaned forward as if dying to give him a hug.

After Bianca left, I sat there for a few seconds. Daniel reached over and touched my hand.

"Something on your mind?"

"She seems quite taken with you."

Daniel chuckled. "She's just ambitious and wants to stay in good with the boss."

"I think it's more than that. I'd say she's interested in you."

"'Interested'?" Daniel said with a laugh. "She's only a young girl."

"Maybe to you. But in her mind she's a full-grown

woman, so don't be naïve. What she's thinking about is more than reporting."

He shook his head, blushing slightly. "Don't be silly. I'd never let anything like that happen."

"Maybe not. But that's what she's planning."

"She just looks up to me as her mentor," he said, stubbornness creeping into his voice.

I stood and looked down on him.

"A lot of mentorships have led to other things. I'm just warning you to be careful."

Daniel gave me an angry look. "I don't need any warnings. You know I won't let anything happen."

I put a hand on his shoulder. "I know you won't." I gave him a peck on the cheek and left.

I didn't now whether I was trying to reassure him or myself.

Chapter Four

I walked back to the office, stewing all the way about Daniel and Bianca. How could he be so blind to something that was so obvious? Or was he really not blind at all, but actually reveling in being fawned upon by an attractive young woman? I knew lots of men who were like that, but I thought Daniel was different. My thoughts swirled angry and black about that subject for the next few blocks, and then I began to chide myself for being so doubting.

I'd met Daniel six months ago when I'd dropped in at *The Sentinel* to place an ad. I'd never tried a newspaper advertisement for myself before, relying on the ones placed by the agency, but business had been kind of slow, and I figured it could only help. While I was going over the details with Myra, he had happened to come out of his office and recognized me from the time a few years before when I had received the Mayor's Award for Heroism. He wasn't living in Minton at the time, but he still read *The Sentinel* faithfully. We had started to chat, and he'd called me a few days later. We'd been going out steadily since then and had even talked in a tentative sort of way about moving in together.

We hadn't acted on it yet for several reasons. I've always been slow to make commitments. I wouldn't say I'm commitment phobic, more just commitment reluctant. I liked my own company and living by myself, so I was comfortable with the way things were. Daniel would like things to have moved on to the next level, but his mother was quite conservative, and he worried about her reaction to our living together without the benefit of marriage. I believe she would adjust easily and be thrilled that he had taken the next step toward having a family. But Daniel was very protective of her and afraid to rock the boat. And although I may have heard wedding bells in my future, I didn't spend every waking moment envisioning my walk down the aisle. So things stayed pretty much as they were.

All this was to say that in the six months we'd been together, he had been kind, attentive, and thoughtful. I've also come to admire his dedication to journalism and his concern for his mother. He'd never given me any reason to doubt him. So, by the time I had made it back to the office, I had convinced myself that I was getting entirely too worked up over this Bianca thing, and I should have more faith in Daniel to handle it tactfully.

"Hi," I said to Molly Cummings, who was covering the phones that afternoon. We each took turns on phone duty during the week according to a strict schedule created weekly by Maggie Fuller, who owned the agency. "Any calls for me?"

She shook her head. "It's been deader than dead," she said, waving the magazine she was reading in my direction. "Just like business in general. Do you have much going on?"

"I had a closing this morning, and I'm still working with the Hastings."

"Lucky you for having a closing. Are the Hastings the couple that fights all the time?"

"That would be the one."

"I heard them going at it once when they were here to see you. I don't know how you put up with them."

"It's just part of the business."

"I suppose. I wonder how they manage to stay together, being so nasty to each other all the time. My husband and I have our disagreements, but they don't last very long. And we always enjoy the making up." Molly gave me a wink.

"Maybe the Hastings enjoy that part," I suggested.

Molly shook her head. "Hard to imagine. They probably fight then, too. They both want to be on top."

I smiled and drifted over to my desk, which is in the front window of the office. Maggie had hired me and paid for my realtor's training because I was a minor celebrity in town. Lots of people knew my name and what I looked like, so she was determined to put me on display. At first, I'd felt exposed and a little embarrassed, but now I enjoyed the perk of having a direct view out on the Minton town green, which was beautiful in all seasons of the year. A quintessential New England scene, I knew it was a spot that lots of people would kill to have as a work location.

All the talk with Molly about the Hastings reminded me that I had promised them I'd keep up to date on any offerings that might fit their parameters. So I fired up my computer and checked the multiple listings, hoping against hope that something new would appear. Luck was with me. A Victorian in the center of town had just come on the market. The listing described the kitchen and baths as having been extensively renovated but was a bit vague as to when this improvement had taken place. In my experience, a number of nineteenth-century homes had been fixed up in the sixties and seventies, which meant that they had sacrificed all their traditional charm and now simply looked outdated and sorely in need of another makeover. The few pictures on the website made it hard to tell whether that was the case here. The house had three floors with seven bedrooms and three baths. That seemed like enough space to keep even the Hastings from each other's throats.

Since I seemed to remember that during one lull in the carping and criticizing, Marcie Hastings had expressed an interest in seeing a Victorian and Roger hadn't immediately interrupted with a sarcastic remark, I figured this offering might be worth a look. I made several telephone calls and managed to arrange a showing for tomorrow evening. I called Roger Hastings and set it up. Nighttime isn't the best for seeing a house, but the Hastings both worked—I pitied their co-workers—so this was our only opportunity. When I was done, I packed my stuff, said goodbye to Molly, and headed home. This was Wednesday night, the night I had dinner at my parents' house, and I wanted time to take a nap and prepare my soul.

Chapter Five

"Have more mashed potatoes," my father said, handing the bowl filled with fluffy white carbohydrates and butter in my direction.

To avoid temptation, I quickly passed them along to my mother who sent them on their way to my younger sister, Amanda, on the other side of the table. Amanda, predictably, put a large scoop on her plate. Although tall and slender—I'd run cross country and played basketball in high school—I still watched my weight the way a bomb disposal expert keeps a careful eye on an armed device, just waiting for it to explode. Amanda, on the other hand, a few inches shorter and considerably more curvaceous than myself, had played softball and field hockey. She also ate as if her seventeen-year-old metabolism would last forever. I admired her optimism.

When we'd finished dessert, an apple pie of which my sister had taken two pieces, my father pushed himself back from the table and patted his ample girth. He was a high school English teacher, so his job was rather sedentary, and given that his eating habits resembled my sister's, I worried whether he would still be around for retirement. I'd tried broaching the subject with my mother, whose excellent cooking made her at least an enabler, but she would only shrug with the hopeless smile of those unwilling to confront an addict.

"As you know," my father began in the firm voice he used in the classroom, "your sister is intent on becoming a police officer."

I nodded, keeping a neutral expression. I'd heard this before—many times. I couldn't get over Amanda's decision. Growing up, she had never modeled herself on me in any way. In fact, I often felt that she made her decisions based upon doing what I wouldn't do. Ten years apart in age, we were never close enough to really fight, and although I'm sure we loved each other in that messy way that siblings do, we generally went our separate ways with the clear implication that the other person was completely misguided. Now she had suddenly decided to follow in my career footsteps. I couldn't help thinking it was some kind of a trick.

"However," my father continued, "Amanda has now also informed us that she does not wish to attend a four-year college. Instead, she wants to study criminal justice at a community college."

"It will save you lots of money, I thought you'd be happy," Amanda said in a hurt tone as if her self-sacrifice was grossly unappreciated.

Dad shook his head. "A community college may give you an adequate preparation for a career, but it is not a complete *education*. You need the broad background that a four-year college education will give you in order to be prepared for the future. Who knows how many career changes you'll have to make in your lifetime, and the better prepared you are, the easier those transitions will be."

"What do you think, Kate?" Mom interrupted. She could tell that Dad was getting warmed up for one of his lectures and wanted to head him off.

I sighed. I hated to be drawn into arguments with my sister. "Many police officers have four-year degrees," I said. "At some time in the future, it will probably be a requirement."

"But it isn't yet," Amanda said. "And I can always go back to college if it becomes necessary."

"It's much harder to return to school once you're working," Dad pointed out.

"And a four-year degree hasn't helped Kate much," Amanda said. "The job she's got now doesn't require any college at all."

I knew that was coming. With Amanda, you're either on her side or not. If you're not, the gloves immediately come off.

"I'm sure having a college degree makes it easier for Kate to talk with people from all walks of life, which she has to do in her job," my mother said. That earned her a scornful glance from Amanda.

"I'm sure I'll learn more from working as a cop than I'll ever get from those two extra years of college. Isn't that true?" Amanda asked, looking at me.

"I'll grant you that there's no substitute for field experience."

"How many times have you used what you learned in those courses in English, history, and science that you had to take?" she asked.

"That's hard to answer," my father interrupted. "That learning is part of who she is, and I'm sure it determines how Kate responds to every situation in both her working and personal life."

Amanda grunted her disdain.

My mother leaned forward and stretched out her arms as if about to make a plea.

"I just don't understand why the two of you want to be on the police force in the first place. I can tell you that I sleep a lot better at night now that Kate has a nice safe job, and I'm not looking forward to having another daughter out there on the streets."

I smiled to myself at the thought of Amanda and myself taking up a life of prostitution.

"And," my mother continued. "Kate certainly wasn't treated very well by the police department. The chief was positively terrible to her."

"Well, I wouldn't want to be on the force here anyway. Minton is just too pokey. I want to be where something is happening," Amanda said.

That was something a little time on the job would get out of her system.

"Just as well," Dad said. "Everybody in town would always be comparing you to Kate. It would make things difficult for you."

Amanda turned red. "And what did she ever do that was so great? She just happened to be in the right place at the right time and did what anybody would have done."

"When you've done something as brave as your sister did, that saved as many lives, then maybe—just maybe—you can talk like that. But until then, I expect you to show your sister some respect."

My father rarely got angry, but this time there was iron in his voice. Amanda blushed a deep red and pushed herself away from the table. A few seconds later we heard the door to her room slam.

"I don't know what gets into her sometimes," my mother said shaking her head.

"Probably hearing too much about me," I said.

My father nodded and sighed. "I should be easier on her. It must have been hard having a sister become a local hero just as you're turning thirteen. It's difficult enough figuring out who you are as a teenager without being compared to a celebrity sister."

"Only a celebrity within five square miles," I said.

"But that was the neighborhood where Amanda spent all her time," Dad said.

I nodded.

"She should go into another field, one where she wouldn't be competing directly with you," he said.

"Telling her that would just make her more determined to be a cop," I said.

"Why can't she go into finance like your brother?" Mom moaned.

Dad and I both grinned at the thought of the wild, aggressive Amanda doing anything like my buttoned down, older brother George, who managed an investment fund in Boston. He was also married to a plain, serious girl who worked as an accountant and was also to all appearances a very capable mother to their two children. All this made him perfect in my mother's book.

"They're different people," my father pointed out gently.

I knew he'd always felt that George, who had studied business, was a bit lacking in imagination and spirit. I whimsically suspected George of being a changeling and thought my real brother was out there somewhere raising hell.

"George never gave us any trouble. He did well in school, got a good job, got married..." Mom continued.

"And had two children," I said.

I had heard the resume of perfect George many times before.

"When are you going to marry that nice man, Daniel, and have some children?" Mom asked.

"Don't push her, Mother, there are already too many failed marriages in the world," Dad said.

"They wouldn't fail. They'd make a wonderful couple," she insisted.

"You never know," I said gaily, "it may happen some day."

"You aren't getting any younger," Mom warned.

"I saw an obituary in today's *Sentinel* for Professor Teller. Wasn't he a teacher of Daniel's?" Dad asked, skillfully changing the subject.

"A teacher and friend."

"The obituary said that his death was a result of a fall. Do you know if he had an accident in the home?"

"Those are so common," Mom added.

I explained that Professor Teller had fallen from his office window.

"Well, then, that was an odd way to express it in the article," my father, ever the English teacher, pointed out.

"The police wanted *The Sentinel* to keep it vague because his death is part of an ongoing investigation. They didn't want the story to give too much away."

"There's a difference between vague and misleading." My father shot me a suspicious glance. "You seem to know an awful lot about what appears to be a police matter."

I could have shrugged it off and remained silent, but eventually a story would be coming out over my byline. My parents would be hurt if they thought I was keeping something from them, so I explained my involvement in the investigation.

"You shouldn't get involved in this, even for Daniel's sake," my mother said. "It will just suck you back into police work."

I smiled. "I don't think there's any chance that the chief will ever suck me back on the force, even if I solve the murder single-handedly."

"I've heard from people who had Teller in class that he was an irascible man but a brilliant teacher. I'm sorry to hear that he's gone. I think you should do whatever you can, within reason, to find out what happened to him," my father said.

"Oh, John, I wish you wouldn't encourage her," Mom said.

"Kate naturally has the nose of a bloodhound," he replied.

I smiled. My father had often told me that as a child, leading to my rushing to stare at my face in the bathroom mirror with rising horror. But I knew myself well enough by now to realize he was right. As much as I had come to accept and even, at times, enjoy my job as a realtor, there was a side of me that still wanted to get to the bottom of things. It was time to put my long nose to the ground.

Chapter Six

I drove home, my mind filled with conflicting thoughts. Why did Amanda really want to be a cop? She liked discipline even less than I did. I was also still stewing over whether Daniel could truly be so blind to Bianca's feelings for him. Most of all I was busy speculating over whether a man in his mid-sixties whose wife had died almost a year ago was likely to be suicidal. My readings in psychology revealed levels of depression increased as people got older, and losing a spouse was one of the most traumatic events in a person's life, but Teller had still been going to work and apparently functioning at a very high level. I didn't want to assume that he had committed suicide without finding out more about his mental state and the on-the-job problems he was supposed to be facing. I hoped my conversation with Dean Messing would give me answers to both of these questions.

I pulled into my parking space outside the converted textile mill along the Minton River where my condominium was located. In the lobby, I grabbed the mail out of my box, and walked up to the third floor and around to the rear of the building. My unit was in the back with a balcony that looked directly out on a bend in the river, offering a dramatic view during all seasons of the year. I'd purchased it when things were going well in the police department, and I had a secure job with a steady, if unspectacular, income. So far I'd managed to make enough through real estate to meet my bills, and Maggie Fuller, the owner of the agency, kept reassuring me that I was good at the job and would only do better as I built up a client base. But it was taking time for me to adjust to the ups and downs of being what was, essentially, an independent entrepreneur. Fortunately, I had my partial pension to fall back on when things got tight.

It was too late to catch the network national news, so I sorted through my mail, which contained nothing but bills and ads, then settled down with my two newspapers: *The Sentinel* and the *Springfield Republican.* Springfield was the nearest large city, and I liked to stay abreast of the news of the area. Knowing what was happening locally was helpful in working with clients and gaining new ones. Tonight, however, I focused on *The Sentinel's* obituary of Joseph Teller. My father had been right. The obituary was highly detailed on Teller's professional accomplishments but rather hazy on his manner of death. He could have fallen from a stepladder in his kitchen or slipped in the shower from all the reader could tell. I knew that by tomorrow Daniel would be pressing Harrington to let him be more specific. A story about a fall from an office window would definitely sell more newspapers although Daniel wouldn't be motivated by such a mercenary motive. He would want to print the truth.

After going through the news carefully, I practiced some yoga poses for half an hour before going to bed. I'd found that they helped a lot since I had spinal fusion three years ago after a drunk driver plowed into the back of my patrol car. Following the yoga with twenty minutes of meditation also put me in the proper frame of mind for sleep.

Sleep came rapidly, but it didn't stay. I was jolted awake at two o'clock, sweating, with my heart beating out of my chest. I'd had the dream again. It had been several months since it had occurred. I sat up in bed and, with a trembling hand, put on the light. As my heart gradually slowed and the trembling lessened, I wondered why it had returned now. The only reason I could come up with was that the conversation around my parents' dinner table had brought back subconscious memories of the event that had made me a local heroine. As with most events that put us in a heroic light, they also leave us damaged.

I was back in the Minton Library again, having just returned some books to the counter and exchanged a few words with Detective Harrington's wife who was working the desk. I turned to my right and headed across the marble foyer to the front door. The ornate metal door opened, and he walked in, carrying, as he had in real life, a canvas bag in his right hand and something in his left. His eyes were half-closed as if he had just awakened from a nap. He had a scruffy beard, and a partially buttoned flannel shirt hanging over baggy jeans.

We were less than six feet apart when he looked up, and that's when it registered with me that he was carrying a rifle. A smile flitted across his face, and he slowly—ever so slowly—raised the barrel, and brought it around in my direction. If I'd been in uniform he might have been faster, but he was enjoying the experience of inflicting terror, watching my eyes to see the fear.

After an instant of disbelief, my training set in. I crossed the distance between us in one long stride and pulled the rifle from his hands. His eyes opened wide as I brought the butt down on the bridge of his nose. He dropped to his knees, and I hit him again—this time strengthened by anxiety and rage—with a solid blow to the temple. He collapsed on his face, and I cuffed him.

It was all over in ten seconds, ten seconds that changed my life forever. That was the way it happened in real life. In my dream, I'm a second too late. I hear the stream of barks from an automatic weapon and feel my body being flung backward across the lobby to lie crumpled against the granite wall. I awake with my diaphragm tight, my abdominal muscles sucked in enough to press against my backbone.

Although today he'd be branded a domestic terrorist, back then he was simply a local wacko, somebody with a long arrest record for assault and burglaries. He lived by himself in a broken down camper and was a dropout from the mental health system. When they opened his bag, they found two handguns, extended clips for the rifle, and some crude pipe bombs. His obvious plan was to mete out as much death and mayhem in the library as possible.

The department at first was very supportive of my actions. They even insisted, much against my wishes, that I appear on the national morning news to describe the event, and for a few days, I was a countrywide phenomenon. Some of the enthusiasm started to diminish when the mayor insisted on awarding me a newly created Minton Citizen Heroism Award. His wife having been among the patrons of the library, she had apparently twisted his arm for me to be recognized for saving so many lives. Word was slowly leaked out from department sources, no doubt directly from the office of Joshua Randal, the chief of police, who never liked to share acclaim, that I had done nothing more than any police officer would have done. I was labeled a media hound with a radical feminist agenda. From then on Chief Randal rarely talked to me or even looked in my direction, and I knew he had revenge on his mind.

Things settled back into place over time, although people on the street who hardly knew me still stopped to say hello. The possibility of being gunned down while taking out a book had clearly captured the local imagination. The chief's opportunity for revenge came over a year later, after I was rear-ended by the drunk and had my back surgery.

For the first six months after I was off rehab, I was on desk duty. That seemed reasonable, and I worked hard at making a full recovery. And at the end of the six months, my surgeon and primary care physician both said that I was capable of returning to active duty. I duly applied. The chief demanded that I be examined by a police doctor who was an old friend of his and who found me unfit for duty. I filed an appeal. The day after I appealed Randal sidled up to me when no one else was in the office.

"Appeal all you want, Cameron, you're going to be behind that desk as long as I'm chief or until the day you die, whichever comes first. So you may as well quit."

After several days of wallowing in anger and outrage, I settled down and considered my options. An endless series of appeals with mixed results didn't seem to be a very productive avenue, but I was damned if I was going to quit. I decided instead to perform a little judo and use the chief's strengths against him, so I applied for early retirement on the grounds of physical disability and cited his doctor's results. My retirement was approved, and I received a very nice partial pension. Again, Chief Randal never forgave me, but now I was safely removed from his power.

Perhaps what had brought the dream back was that for the first time since leaving the force, I was nibbling around the edges of a possible crime, and bringing myself once again into conflict with the chief. I considered that for a long moment. I could easily explain the situation to Daniel, and I was sure he'd understand and be willing to let me end my involvement with the Teller story, especially since Bianca seemed to be doing such a fine job on her own.

I imagined the smug smile on her face when she heard that she'd no longer have to share a byline with me. That would just embolden her to set her cap for Daniel. If Bianca thought she'd run me off once, she'd decide she could easily do it again. I wasn't about to give her that kind of encouragement. Also, when it came to the chief, I'd never taken a step backward when confronted by him before, so why should I start now? A few bad dreams wouldn't kill me, and once you start living primarily to avoid conflict, you're on a road that never ends. Minton was too small a town for me to completely avoid the chief; our paths were bound to cross eventually. I should face it with the same determination that I'd faced everything else in my life. After giving myself that little pep talk, I rolled over and easily went back to sleep.

Chapter Seven

"Everybody has their clients from hell. Only once have I dropped a couple for bad behavior, and they got into a physical fight in a home we were viewing and knocked a Dresden clock off a mantelpiece. I had to cover the cost. I told them they needed a referee, not a real estate agent."

Nancy Bryant chuckled at her own joke and leaned back far enough in her swivel chair to make it squeak. A gruff old Yankee who had been a realtor for over twenty years—since her husband passed away and left her with two kids to raise—she was a source of wisdom for me.

"Did you notice the obituary in *The Sentinel* about that professor who died up at the university?" I asked.

She shook her head. "I subscribe to *The Sentinel*, but, no offense to your boyfriend, I hardly ever read it. Usually, I know what's happening in town before it ever gets into print."

"Well, Daniel has me looking into the death. I'm sort of working as a reporter on the story."

Nancy raised an eyebrow. "Boyfriends get us to do the strangest things, don't they?"

"It seems this Professor Teller lost his wife about a year ago, so the police think he might have committed suicide by jumping from his office window. Daniel really wants to know the truth."

Nancy stared at the ceiling thoughtfully. "I suppose everybody is different, but I was pretty much coming out of my funk by the end of a year. Of course, I had two boys to look after, so I didn't have the luxury of doing much brooding. I had to be both the cheerleader and breadwinner. But I guess I would have expected this professor to kill himself sooner if he was going to do it."

I nodded. "I thought the same thing. Plus I wondered about jumping from a third-floor window as a method of suicide. It just doesn't seem very reliable."

"And don't men usually prefer guns, while women use pills? I guess women think it's like falling asleep, and they'll be beautiful corpses."

"From the pictures I've seen, that's not true."

"Dead is dead. How beautiful can it be?"

As if on cue, the front door opened and Maggie Fuller, the owner of The Colonial Real Estate Agency, made her entrance. As usual, she was impeccably dressed in a finely tailored suit. Every hair was in place and her makeup created the artificially perfect complexion expected from someone who had spent most of her time in front of a camera. Although she rarely referred to it, Maggie had once been a television hostess and pitch person on a local Boston station. It had apparently been a formative period in her life because she always looked ready for her close-up.

Her looks were more aristocratic than pretty. Her long nose and high cheekbones gave her an elegance somewhat out of place in Minton. Between that and her clothes, she attracted attention wherever she went, which probably pleased her.

"Good morning everyone," she announced, as

though the office were crowded with people instead of there being only Nancy and myself. "Are we doing a lot of business today?"

Although the question sounded casual, when it involved work, Maggie always expected an answer.

"I have a showing tonight," I said.

"I'm meeting a client this afternoon. I'm covering the phones right now," Nancy added.

"Good, good," Maggie murmured, not delaying in her progress to her office in the back of the building.

"The queen," Nancy said after she heard Maggie's office door close.

I shrugged. "I've worked for worse."

"I can't remember the last time she actually sold a house herself."

"Why should she? She gets a cut of each one we sell."

"Doesn't seem right. We do all the work, and she reaps the benefits," Nancy said.

"But she has to cover the costs of running the agency out of that."

Nancy frowned. "How much does the rent on this office amount to? We're in the middle of Minton, not in the heart of Boston. And she does most of her advertising in *The Sentinel*, which, apologies to your boyfriend again, isn't exactly the *New York Times*."

I smiled. "Sounds like you should buy your own agency and run it."

"Maybe at one time, I'm too old now. I do well enough with what I make here. But if I were you, I'd be thinking about going out on my own. With your local reputation, you'd be a big success."

"Maggie would kill me."

Nancy chuckled. "She might at that. But seriously, you should give it some thought. Within the next ten years, Minton is going to really develop. You could make a killing."

"If I decide to stay in real estate, maybe I'll do just that."

I checked my watch. It was time for me to leave for my appointment with the dean.

* * * *

Dean Messing squinted at me as if trying to recall where he had seen me before. He'd invited me into his office after a short wait. He was a large fleshy man with a severe crew cut that made him look like an ex-marine who had started to go to seed. We were sitting across from each other in a couple of wingback chairs off to the side of his desk. I figured he wanted to give the impression of being more open and informal when meeting with the press. His face cleared, and I knew he'd remembered who I was.

"You're the police officer who apprehended that man who was planning to shoot all those people in the Minton Library."

I nodded.

"That was admirable work—very admirable."

"Thank you."

"But you said you're a reporter."

"I left the force on a partial disability two years ago. Now I sell real estate and help out occasionally at *The Sentinel*." The last part was a bit of an exaggeration, but I didn't want him to know this was my first journalistic effort. I had purchased a small spiral notebook that I had open on my lap to give me credibility. I hoped it was enough.

50

"I see. Well, I'm afraid there isn't much I can tell you that I haven't already mentioned to the police. Joe was, of course, an important part of our Minton State University family. He'd taught here for almost twenty years, ever since leaving a career in journalism in Boston. We were very fortunate to have him."

I stared at the beige carpet. It was a soothing room with tan walls and earth tone furniture. It reminded me of an airport or a doctor's waiting room.

"I gather Professor Teller had some tragedy in his life recently."

"You mean the death of his wife. Yes, it was cancer, slow and very painful. It was a harrowing experience for Joe, but he kept on teaching a full course load all through it. He was a real trouper."

"But yet you think he committed suicide?"

The dean shrugged his large shoulders. "Everyone has a breaking point."

"A year after her death seems like a funny time to break."

Dean Messing stared hard at me. He clearly didn't care for my close questioning.

"Who can tell how people are going to react to grief? I can only assume that for Joe it built up over time until it became unbearable."

"Was that his only problem? I understand that Professor Teller had some career issues."

Messing frowned. "I'm sorry the police saw fit to share that information with the public. That should have remained confidential. I certainly wouldn't want it to get into print. Joe was a good man, and I wouldn't want anything disparaging about his work to get out there."

"So there were some career issues?"

"Although he came to class every day and continued to teach, I would have to say that his enthusiasm for his work declined in the year after his wife's death. His student evaluations weren't quite as stellar, he stopped attending professional conferences, and he wasn't working on any scholarly articles."

"According to our records, Professor Teller was sixty-seven. Did you try to pressure him to retire?"

"Of course not, that would be a serious breach of the law," he said sharply. "I simply pointed out to him that his energy level didn't seem to be what it once was."

"But it was only a year after his wife's death. It doesn't seem as though you were cutting him much slack."

The dean pursed his lips as if to hold back an angry retort. He clearly didn't like implied criticism any more than close questioning.

"Don't get me wrong. I wasn't threatening him. I met with Joe primarily to offer him advice and counseling. That's one of my roles as Dean. I have to encourage faculty as well as admonish them."

"And you encouraged Professor Teller by giving some of his courses to…" I looked down at the blank page in my notebook, as if I had to check on the name. "A Professor Rockwell Brody, of whom you are a close personal friend."

Messing stared hard at me again as if trying to interpret my use of the word "personal." I kept a bland expression on my face as though I meant they were just buddies.

He lurched to his feet. "I don't know what you are trying to imply. But at the very least you are suggesting that I would allow my personal feelings to unduly influence my professional judgment. You'd better be careful not to print anything libelous because I assure you that I will sue."

I stood up and looked him in the eye. We were the same height. Once again the inches that had been a curse when I was an adolescent were an advantage as an adult.

"It isn't libelous if it's true."

He blinked slowly, like a reptile. "I also want you to know that I intend to call *The Sentinel* and let them know about the quality of the people they allow to work for them."

I wasn't worried about that; Daniel would field it with the appropriate diplomatic skill.

"You might also be interested to know that Chief Randal is another *personal* friend of mine, and I intend to tell him that you are interfering in a police investigation."

That worried me a bit more.

Chapter Eight

I left the Administration Building and headed over
to the Dillard Building. I wanted to ask some more
questions. I wasn't certain whom I wanted to ask or
exactly what, but I'd learned on the job that sometimes
random, improvised questioning led to surprising
nuggets of information. I went upstairs in Dillard to the
third floor. I went down a long hall until a sign on the
wall said that I had reached the English Department
Office. I walked into a large room with two desks
facing the door. Behind the desk on my left, a tall
young woman, almost my height, was talking to Evan
Miller, the student I had met outside the Dillard
Building the other day.

"Hello, Ms. Cameron," he said, giving me a big
smile and running his hand through his blond hair.
"Still looking for more information for your story?"

"I certainly am," I said. "Do you have anything for
me?"

He shook his head. "I'm not one to go around
asking questions. I stick to my books."

"Just as well." I turned to the young woman who
was watching us with a slightly bewildered smile. "I
just wanted to get some more background information
on Professor Teller."

She stared at me through thick lenses in black
plastic frames, which made her eyes look large and

moist. She stuck her hand out across the desk. "I'm Fiona Halsey. I work as a secretarial intern here in the English Department."

I took her hand. "Then maybe you can help me."

"I should be going now. I have a class in ten minutes," Evan said. "See you around."

"Bye now," Fiona said softly.

"You probably will be seeing me," I replied.

When he left the room, I turned back to Fiona. "He seems like a nice fellow," I said.

She nodded, not willing to take up the subject. "I'm not sure how I can help you. I didn't know Professor Teller that well. I'm an English major, but I haven't taken any journalism courses yet."

I looked at the wall that held a row of mailboxes.

"You must have seen him come in to pick up his mail."

"Once in a while."

"Did he seem happy? In good spirits?"

She shrugged. "He was very businesslike. He never stopped to chat." She leaned across the desk and lowered her voice. "I've heard what people are saying about him committing suicide, but I don't really believe that. Look at these windows," she said, pointing to the one behind her. "See how low they are. Professor Teller was tall, even taller than I am, and I'm always very careful when we have them open. It would be real easy to fall over the edge of the sill."

"So you don't think he jumped?"

"Because his wife died?"

She was about to say more when a trim woman in her forties came into the office and looked at me inquiringly.

"Can I help you?" she asked.

She was obviously the English Department's version of Myra Kepler, the anonymous woman who kept the Department running.

"I'm doing an in-depth article on Professor Teller for *The Sentinel*, and I wanted to talk to some people who had worked with him."

"I'm Janet Phillips, the Department secretary, so I wouldn't say I *worked with* him. We just provide faculty support. They all pretty much work on their own. The faculty are a bit like independent contractors," she said, smiling at her own wit.

"But you must have seen him on a regular basis over a long period of time."

"I've only worked here five years, but I guess I did see him four or five times a week during the semester. We'd exchange a few words about the weather or he'd ask me about the time of a meeting. Nothing personal."

"You were aware that his wife died about a year ago?"

The woman frowned. "Some of the other faculty told me. Professor Teller never mentioned it, and there was no funeral as such."

"Did you notice any change in his mood after her death?"

"He may have been a bit quieter, but that could just be my imagination. He was always rather reserved."

I paused, not sure what to ask next. Suddenly I had an inspiration.

"Did you notice anyone in the hall around the time of Professor Teller's death?"

She gave me a puzzled look.

"I don't see where you're going with this."

I smiled disarmingly. "I was just hoping that maybe someone saw him shortly before his death and would be able to tell me more about his state of mind."

At first, I thought she was going to refuse to answer, then she relented.

"Did you notice anyone in the hall, Fiona?"

The girl squinted through her glasses and shook her head.

"Neither did I. Of course, lots of people go past the door in an afternoon. We probably wouldn't pay attention unless it was a stranger. We're supposed to call security if we see anyone suspicious roaming the halls." She sighed. "I'm afraid that's the way things are these days."

"Are all the English Department faculty offices off this hall?"

"Except for a large room where the adjuncts have desks. That's on the next floor up."

"Would you have any way of knowing who might have been in their offices at the time of Professor Teller's death?"

"I have a chart with everyone's posted office hours for the semester. Of course, there's no guarantee that the faculty member actually kept his or her posted hours. Sometimes events intervene."

"I understand."

She walked over to her desk and flipped open a loose-leaf notebook.

"Pretty low tech," I commented.

"So are most of the faculty. It's easier to get them to fill out a sheet of paper than to e-mail me information." She glanced through the pages. "According to this Professor Franks, the Department chairperson, was in her office. That's right next door to this. In fact, I remember seeing her in the hall when security came by to tell us about Professor Teller."

"Anyone else?"

"Professor Boyd was here. But I can't say that I saw him, so he may not have actually been in his office. Some professors are more reliable than others in keeping office hours," she said, suggesting that Boyd was among the irresponsible.

I wondered if being a personal friend of the dean gave you special privileges.

"But Professor Boyd's office is in the front of the building. Professor Teller's was around the side, so they aren't really situated very close together. They probably wouldn't have seen each other."

I smiled. "Thank you for your help."

She nodded briskly.

"Would it be possible for me to make an appointment to talk with the English Department chairperson? She might be able to tell me a bit more about Professor Teller from a professional standpoint."

"You're certainly being very thorough."

"I try."

"I thought that nice obituary in the paper would have been enough."

"The editor of *The Sentinel* is a former student of Professor Teller's, so he wants to go the extra mile."

Janet Phillips checked a calendar on her desk.

"Professor Franks is free tomorrow at ten o'clock. Would that work for you?"

I said it would. "Just one more question. Has anything happened recently that seemed to disturb Professor Teller more than usual?"

The secretary paused. "He did have an appointment with Professor Franks the day before he died. He told me he had a very important matter he wanted to discuss with her."

"But you don't know what it was?"

She shook her head. "Perhaps Professor Franks will tell you tomorrow when you see her."

I nodded, hoping that was true.

When I got back to the car, I called Daniel at *The Sentinel* offices to tell him what I'd learned. He suggested that we get together tonight for dinner and a brainstorming session, but I told him I had to take the Hastings out for a viewing. Although I didn't say it, I didn't think there was much for us to brainstorm about as of yet.

"What is your gut telling you?" Daniel asked. "Do you think it's an accident or suicide?"

"I think it's too soon for my gut to have an opinion," I replied. "Neither an accident or suicide fits the situation precisely, but either is a possibility."

"What about murder?" Daniel said, almost is a whisper.

"Who's your suspect?"

"Dean Messing. He's the one with the motivation. Get Professor Teller out and get his boyfriend in."

"Maybe, but I don't think he'd resort to murder. He's more of an administration in-fighter. He strikes me as the kind of guy who would find some bureaucratic way to get Teller out rather than resorting to violence."

"Professor Teller could be stubborn, and he'd been there a long time. He might have a lot of friends in the faculty and administration. Messing might have decided it would be hard to get rid of him by the normal methods."

"Could be. Have you heard anything more from Bianca?"

"No." There was a long pause. "But I've been giving what you said about Bianca some thought, and I really don't think there's anything to worry about."

"If you say so," I replied.

He paused. I could tell he wasn't happy with my response. "How about we get together for dinner on Saturday night? Would that work?"

I knew he was trying to make things better between us. "Sounds fine."

"Good, I'll pick you up around six-thirty. What's on your agenda for tomorrow?"

I told him about my plan to meet with the chairperson of the English Department.

"How about we get together at *The Sentinel* for a meeting at around four? Sorry to make it so late, but Bianca has classes until then."

"No problem," I said through gritted teeth.

"Fine, see you then."

I tried to sound cheerful as I said goodbye.

Chapter Nine

I got up the next morning and went out for a run. Three times a week I try to get in two miles. Combined with trips to the gym, it's enough to keep me in shape without overstressing my back. I especially needed an endorphin high this morning because my meeting with the Hastings the night before had been challenging, to say the least. The house turned out to be a large white three story Victorian. Marcie liked the scalloped shingles and the wraparound porch, while Roger grumbled about the cost of maintenance, particularly the need for expensive repainting every few years. Both seemed impressed with the oak floors, which appeared to be in good condition, the elaborate moldings, and the elegant center stairway, and they agreed that the large dining room would be excellent for family dinners on holidays. I wondered how many family members actually attended their festivities.

I took them upstairs to see the five bedrooms before going into the kitchen, which my experience with Victorians made me anticipate would require extensive remodeling. The bedrooms were spacious and the master bedroom in the front had actually been remodeled to include a master bathroom, almost unheard of in a house of this age. I actually began to harbor hopes.

The kitchen, as I had suspected, had been

remodeled in the sixties and was sorely in need of a redo. Before they could get on a roll with their complaints, I pointed out that the price of the house was so far below their budget that they could easily afford to gut and replace the kitchen. Then Marcie discovered the stairway from the kitchen to the upstairs.

"Where does this go?" she asked.

"Probably directly up to the third-floor servants' quarters. These houses often had a stairway that only the servants would use."

Marcie insisted on going up. The attic was divided into a number of small chambers.

"This is terrible," she said. "How could people live like this?"

"They were servants," Roger pointed out. "They probably considered themselves lucky to have a job."

She glared at him.

"You wouldn't have to use this space," I said. "According to the listing, it isn't connected to the central heating anyway."

"There's no heat up here. How did people live?" Marcie exclaimed.

"Fireplaces, like everyone else," Roger said, pointing to the small fireplace in each room. "And since when did you have such a social conscience?"

"You should try caring for someone other than yourself for once."

"I'm not the one who spends most of my free time shopping," he shot back.

"I have to do something, you're never around."

"Do you wonder why?"

I tuned out the conversation and led them downstairs. Back in the kitchen, they stopped fighting long enough to agree that the house didn't "tick enough of their boxes." I smiled valiantly and led them outside where I promised to keep looking. By the time they were back in the car, they were arguing again, both of them waving their hands and talking loudly enough that I could hear the hum of voices like angry bees as they drove away.

I promised myself that if no progress had been made when my contract with them ran out at the end of October, I would suggest they find a different agent.

By the time I had run along the river and returned home, I had put most of that behind me. I puttered around the condo, cleaning and straightening until it was time for me to go to the University and see the English Department chairperson. I drove along the streets, bordered by trees starting to show the brightly colored leaves of early fall. It gave every promise of being a typically beautiful season. I parked in my usual visitor's space by the administration building and slowly walked over to Dillard, savoring the atmosphere of the campus.

Janet Phillips got up from behind her desk as I walked into the office.

"Right on time, that's wonderful," she said.

"I admire punctuality in others and try to practice it myself."

She nodded and lowered her voice. "I do as well, but sadly students and faculty often have a much looser sense of time."

We gave each other conspiratorial grins. She took me outside into the hall and knocked on the next door. A woman's voice called for us to come in. Janet opened the door, and a trim woman with short black hair rose from the chair behind the desk. She reached out a thin hand with several rings on it, none of them a wedding ring, and shook my hand as Janet performed the introductions.

"I'm Jessica Franks. It's good to know that Joe will be properly appreciated in the community," she said, motioning to the only other chair in the room as the secretary gently closed the door behind her.

"The editor of *The Sentinel* was a student of Professor Teller's, and he was very influenced by him," I explained.

"A lot of journalism students were. There are many reporters and people in communications out there in their thirties and early forties who were mentored by him. He knew newspapers and had a dynamic personality."

We chatted for a few minutes about Teller's academic contributions. Then I decided it was time to get down to business.

"But I gather from Dean Messing that he'd been a bit subdued as of late."

Jessica Franks frowned when I mentioned the dean's name.

"Joe was certainly upset by his wife's death. Who wouldn't be? They'd been married for forty years. He may have been a bit down for a while, but it never affected his teaching."

I decided to go in hard. "That isn't what the dean said. He suggested that he'd had to give some of Professor Teller's courses to Professor Boyd." The dean hadn't exactly told me that. In fact, I'd told him that based on Bianca's secret source, but he hadn't denied it, so I figured it was close enough to the truth.

Professor Frank's mouth formed a tight line. "The dean shouldn't be sharing that kind of information about the department. And it's not completely true. There was nothing wrong with Joe's teaching. Everyone has ups and downs on student evaluations. It's all open to interpretation."

"The dean just had a preference for Professor Boyd?"

She gave me a long stare, probably wondering how much I knew about the men's personal relationship.

"I got the impression the dean wouldn't have been unhappy to have Professor Teller retire," I continued.

"I fail to see how any of this is relevant to the article you plan to write on Joe," she said in a cold tone.

I wasn't sure how to proceed, but I had a feeling that giving her a bit of the truth as to my motivation might be wise.

"My contact on the police force says that they are unsure as to how Professor Teller came to fall out that window. In my article, I don't want to suggest that he jumped unless we are quite sure as to his motivations. Being pressured by the dean to retire might have contributed to his desire to jump."

Professor Franks ran a hand over her forehead.

"I find it hard to believe Joe committed suicide, but no other alternative seems likely. And yes, he was under some pressure from the dean. He was never explicitly asked to retire, but the implication that it would be looked upon favorably was certainly there." She paused and gave me a crooked smile. "Can I speak off the record?"

I nodded.

"The University has had some budget problems

with the State recently, and we haven't received our funding for the usual number of positions in English. Rockwell Boyd is up for tenure next year, and from everything I know, he is certainly qualified to receive it; however, we simply don't have a tenured position for him."

"So what will happen?"

Franks shrugged. "We may have to let him go. Possibly the administration could give him a one-year contract, while he looked for another position, but the outcome probably wouldn't be good for him."

"So the dean, being his friend, was trying to get Professor Teller out, so Boyd could have his tenured slot?"

"The dean never actually said this, but it's my interpretation of his actions."

I stared across the room at the shelves of books that filled one wall. I wondered, as I had always done when sitting in the offices of my professors, whether she had read them all.

"What was your position on all this? Did you favor replacing Teller with Boyd?"

"Boyd is certainly talented and Joe could sometimes be a bit old line. He came to me the day before he died all fired up about a possible case of plagiarism. He thought someone had submitted a story stolen from the Internet. I guess those who have worked in journalism are very sensitive to that sort of thing. I told him to use one of those search engines that hunts down the use of unattributed information and make sure of his facts."

"Who was the student?"

"He didn't want to say without proof. He had the

paper in his hand but didn't show it to me. He stood in the hallway and virtually shouted that this sort of thing couldn't be allowed."

"So, if Teller was so unreasonable, were you in favor of giving Boyd the position?" I pressed.

"I didn't say that," she snapped. "Don't put words in my mouth. I don't like administrators giving favors to friends. Decisions should be based as much as possible on merit. So what the dean was doing made me very uncomfortable. But I also would have been sorry to see Boyd let go."

"Someday you may find that the dean is grooming Boyd for your position."

Her eyes narrowed and became hard. "He would be very unwise to attempt that."

I had a feeling that the dean's *personal friendship* would become very public if he tried to replace Jessica Franks.

"Do you think that the pressure just became too great for Professor Teller and he jumped?"

"I wouldn't have thought so. He was a pretty tough guy. Although the last time we talked, he rambled a bit and started talking about how things weren't the way they used to be."

"In what way?"

"The students, mostly, I think. He felt they weren't as serious as they once were. At the time I thought he sounded disgruntled, the way so many older faculty do right before they decide to retire. But maybe..." She waved a hand.

"Maybe he was considering something more final."

She sighed. "Aside from a psychiatrist, whoever expects that the person sitting across from her is truly suicidal? I thought he was just a little down in the dumps about this plagiarism thing and being under pressure from the dean."

"Maybe that was all it was."

"You don't seriously think this was an accident and that he fell."

"There is another alternative."

The professor thought for a minute, then her eyes opened wide.

"You're not talking about...murder?"

"It's a possibility."

"A pretty remote one, I'd say. I certainly can't think of anyone who would want to kill Joe. And I would suggest that before you put something like that in your article you'd better run it by the police and then make sure *The Sentinel* has a good lawyer."

I smiled as I stood. "Don't worry, it's too early to be making accusations like that. I'd appreciate it if you'd keep it under your hat."

She stood and faced me. "I've already forgotten that I ever heard it."

We shook hands, and I left.

As I walked back to the car, I reflected on my conversation. I'd brought up the possibility of murder just to see her reaction. Sometimes a momentary hesitation or a slight gesture will indicate that the idea isn't too far off base. However, Franks seemed to reject it out of hand and without reservation. I was starting to feel the same way myself. Even though Daniel had felt that Teller wasn't despondent, the evidence indicated he had some reason to be. Suicide certainly seemed the more likely answer than either accident or murder.

Just as I was about to get in the car, my phone

rang. It was Detective Dennis Harrington.

"Just thought you'd like to know that Chief Randal has gotten the word of your involvement in this investigation."

"Dean Messing?"

"Called the chief yesterday afternoon. Randal ran into my office right afterward madder than a wet hen."

"No one likes civilians getting involved in police business."

"I think it's the particular civilian involved that bothers him. He still holds a grudge, you know."

"I know."

"I told him you were working for the newspaper, and I couldn't keep you from investigating the story. He wasn't happy about that, but I guess he couldn't think of any way to stop you."

"I'm sure he's giving it lots of thought."

"So if the dean is so upset, you must have found out something. Maybe we should get together and talk about it."

"Do you think that's wise? The chief would make your life pretty miserable if he knew we were working together."

"I was a detective before he was chief, and I bet I'll still be a detective long after he's gone."

"Sure, but I don't want to be responsible for wrecking your career. How about we meet outside of town where no one in the department is likely to spot us?"

"North Minton?" Harrington said.

Although it was only ten miles from the center of Minton, we both knew that no members of the force would be caught hanging out up there. It might as well have been on the other side of the state.

"What about Rachel's Diner on Main Street?"

"Sounds fine. How about noon?"

Once we had agreed, I got in my car and drove back to the office. I still had some time to devote to my favorite activity, finding a home for the Hastings.

Chapter Ten

I parked on the street about a block past Rachel's. As I walked back I saw the black sedan that belonged to Harrington right near the door. He must have gotten there early because the noon crowd had nearly filled in the street parking in front of the place. I walked in and spotted him in a booth by the front window.

I went up to the table and shook his hand. He already had a burger and fries in front of him. He apologized and told me he was on a tight schedule.

"I expected you to have a spot in the back and be wearing a wig and glasses," I said.

He gave me a grudging smile. "Don't think I didn't consider it. Sitting down with you is like meeting with a known terrorist, according to the chief."

I slid into the booth. "It's good to be appreciated."

A waitress hurried over, and I put in an order for a tuna on rye and coffee.

"What do you have for me?" I asked when she left.

"You go first. I'm the one taking all the risk."

I filled him in on the relationship between Dean Messing and Rockwell Boyd and told him how this had led to a conflict between Messing and Teller. When I was through, he took a big bite out of his burger and chewed thoughtfully.

"Do you think that Messing or Boyd might have done something drastic if Teller threatened to go public about their relationship in order to keep his job?"

I hadn't really considered that. I felt stupid for a moment and could see why Harrington was the detective. Sometimes I forget that I was never more than a beat cop and later a desk jockey, then suddenly something like this brings me back to earth.

"I don't know for a fact that Teller was aware of their relationship."

"If your student snitch, Bianca, could find out about it in a few hours, I bet most of the faculty and administration knows."

I smiled at the idea of Bianca being called a snitch. I kind of liked the image. "You're right, of course. Teller most likely did know about it, and if the dean leaned on him hard enough to retire, he could have threatened to blow the whistle. That would very likely ruin the dean's career as well as Boyd's, giving them both a motive for murder.

"I think I'll have another little talk with the dean tomorrow and find out where he was at the time Teller took his fall. I've already interviewed Boyd because he was on the same floor as Teller at the time of the incident. He claims not to have heard anything, but this new information gives him both motive and opportunity."

Harrington paused and frowned.

"What's wrong?" I asked.

"I take it you haven't met this fellow Boyd?"

I shook my head.

"Well, there's one problem with liking him for the murder, he's a small guy. I'm not sure I see him being able to wrestle a big, tall fellow like Teller out a window, even if Boyd is a lot younger."

"He could have caught him by surprise."

"That's always possible."

"If you don't mind, I'd like to have a chat with him myself. I could say I was looking for further background for my piece on Teller."

"That's going to be quite a story."

I smiled. "Epic."

"Go ahead and talk to him, but try not to get him so angry that he calls the chief."

"The dean may call again himself when he hears that I talked to his boyfriend."

"No problem. Once I fill the chief in on Messing's involvement in all this, he might not be so inclined to listen to him."

My sandwich came and I dug into it. I'm a hearty eater, and I don't put on any feminine pretense by picking at my food. Within a couple of minutes, half the sandwich was gone.

"So what have you got for me?" I asked, wiping my mouth with a napkin.

"Going through the contacts on his phone, we found out that Teller had a girlfriend, a woman named Marge Rowen. I interviewed her. "

"If he was involved in a new relationship, that would lessen the chances that he committed suicide. He sounds like he was starting over in life."

"Right. But it does increase the chances that it might have been murder."

"How's that?" I asked around my second half of sandwich.

"Marge has a jealous ex. Teller apparently already had one confrontation with the guy."

"What's his name?"

"Owen Dragmore. Apparently, Marge took back her maiden name after they broke up. He's been arrested several times for getting into bar fights. He's generally a bad piece of work."

"Was Teller hurt in this confrontation?"

Harrington shook his head. "Apparently, it didn't go beyond some threats and shouting. But it worried Marge enough that she got a restraining order against the guy. We had a chat with him, and he claims to have been at work at the time of Teller's death. We called the shop, and they confirmed it. But who knows? I keep hoping he'll come around and bother her, so we can bring Dragmore in and really grill him."

"Guys like that are pretty tricky. They know just enough of the law to be dangerous. If you don't mind, I'd like to have a talk with her as well. Maybe Marge will share something with a woman that she might not have mentioned to you."

"Would this be for the massive story you're writing on Teller?"

"That's the one."

"Okay, just let me know if you find out anything new."

He gave me her address and phone number, and I wrote them down.

"Anything else?" I asked.

"Would you mind listening to someone who's a lot older and has handled a few more investigations than you have?"

"I'm always willing to take good advice."

Harrington nodded and speared his last French fry. "I know there's some reason to believe that Teller might have been murdered, but it still fits the profile of a suicide more than a murder. Pushing a guy from a third-floor window doesn't show much planning, and it certainly runs a high risk of getting caught. If it was murder, it would have to be pretty impulsive."

"Yes. Performed by somebody who was highly emotional and really stressed."

"Right, probably following a fight of some sort."

"But nobody heard anything," I pointed out. "Boyd was the only one at that end of the floor, and he was around toward the front of the building. The sounds might not have traveled that far, although you'd think a good loud fight would echo all around that old building. And, of course, that's assuming it wasn't Boyd himself who did it."

"Which is possible. All I'm saying is don't go running off down the murder road too quickly. Try to take a balanced approach. Even if Teller had a girlfriend that doesn't mean he wasn't pining for his wife. Grief can be there on the inside even if someone seems normal."

I remembered with a jolt that Harrington and his wife had lost a son in Afghanistan a few years ago, so likely he knew what he was talking about.

"Thanks for the advice. I will definitely keep it in mind."

He nodded and smiled. "Keep up the good work and stay in touch."

"I'll try not to get you in too much trouble with the chief."

"That's probably not possible, so don't worry. I'll take care of it."

I nodded, not sure whether he could.

Chapter Eleven

I gave Marge Rowen a call and presented my pitch about how I was writing an in-depth story about Joseph Teller. She seemed excited by the idea and very eager to help. We agreed that we'd meet at her home in two hours. Since she was on the south side of Minton, I decided to stop in the office to do a little more research on finding a place for the Hastings.

Molly Cummings was covering the phones again. Things must have been slow because she was doing her nails. She waved a limp hand at me as I walked through the door.

"Don't let Maggie catch you doing that," I warned. "She thinks personal beautification should take place on your own time."

"Thanks for the warning," Molly said, slipping the bottle of polish behind a loose-leaf notebook where it couldn't be seen.

I sat at my desk in the front window and brought up the multiple listing service website. I put in the parameters that fit the Hastings and began to scroll. Suddenly I became aware of a large blue presence hovering in front of my desk. I looked up and saw Chief Randal staring down on me. I quickly pushed my chair back from the desk as if confronted by a rabid raccoon.

"Walk with me," he said. Turning, he left the office. He didn't close the door, as if confident that I would follow.

I stood up. A part of me wanted to close the door and ignore him, but another part of me was curious to find out the reason for his visit. I looked over at Molly who had a hand with a brush still poised in the air and was staring at me open-mouthed. I walked around my desk and went outside. Randal was a couple of doors down standing still and not looking back, waiting as if it were inevitable that I would follow. I came up to stand next to him, and we began to walk slowly side by side. In my one-inch heels, we were the same height. We went along like two friends out for a pleasant stroll. He was a good-looking guy in a fiftyish sort of way with regular features, striking blue eyes, and a gray brush cut. He looked like a general who, although now on desk duty, still stayed in combat shape.

"I hear you've gotten involved in the Teller case," he said, staring forward, not bothering to look at me.

"I'm writing an article about it for *The Sentinel*."

"Are you a reporter now?"

"Just doing a favor for a friend."

He nodded. "Daniel Rencardi."

"That's right."

"I don't want you involved in police business. You gave up that right when you retired."

He waited for me to say something, but I didn't.

"Do you like selling real estate?"

"It's okay."

"Well, if I find that you've printed anything that you didn't run past Harrington first, you won't be doing that in Minton anymore."

"You can't frighten Maggie," I said, hoping that was true.

He considered the idea. "Maybe not. But I can have a long influential talk with the owner of *The Sentinel*, and your boyfriend could find himself out on his ear. I hear that newspaper jobs are hard to come by, and I know he wants to stay in Minton to be near his mom. That means he'd have to look for another job in town, and I could make that very tough for him."

He waited for my reply. I knew that anything I said would put me at a disadvantage so I remained silent.

"Anything else?" I finally asked.

He glanced over at me. "Nope, that's all." He nodded and walked over to his car parked by the curb. He'd obviously choreographed this whole conversation to perfection, even to making the well-timed exit. He paused and stared over the roof of the car at me. "You know what I don't like about you?"

Let me make a list, I thought, but I just stared back.

"You're not a team player."

"I should have waited for backup before apprehending the shooter in the library?"

"What happened afterward was the problem."

"You told me to go on television, and I didn't have a choice about accepting the mayor's award."

"I misjudged how that would work out. It meant a permanent change in your position in the department." He looked away for a moment as if reviewing what he could have done differently. "Do you garden?"

I shook my head.

"Well, sometimes you'll put the same kind of plants in a garden, and for some reason, one or two will tower over all the rest. You might think that's a good thing, but it spoils the effect of the entire garden. You know what you have to do?"

"Cut them down to size?"

"Exactly. That's why you couldn't stay on the force. If you hadn't been in that car accident, I'd have found another way."

I wondered if he'd have handled it the same way if I hadn't been a woman. I didn't ask. I didn't want to give him the satisfaction of accusing me of playing the feminist card.

"That's also a good way to lose your best people," I said.

He shrugged. "It's for the good of the whole. You have to think of the team."

"A team of mediocrities."

A flash of anger passed over his face. He opened the car door and got inside. As he drove away, I took some satisfaction in getting his goat, but I was worried that I'd end up paying for it later.

Chapter Twelve

Marge Rowen's house was a small cape on a street lined with small capes. Popping the roofs with dormers or putting additions on the back had enlarged most of the others and broken up the boring uniformity. Marge's, however, remained exactly as it had been when built in the late nineteen fifties. I speculated that the kitchen and bathroom would also hark back to the same era. Her husband was probably too busy sinking his paycheck into drink to make home improvements. Somebody looking for a starter home could get a good deal by purchasing the place cheap and investing money in updates.

The only signs of careful attention were the two small gardens on either side of the front porch. Although starting to fade with the cooler weather of fall, there was still enough glory there to suggest that they had been ablaze with color during the summer. Marge obviously made an effort within her financial limitations. I rang the bell. A short slight woman opened the door and smiled through the aluminum storm window. She had salt and pepper hair, and a slightly surprised expression as if life constantly kept her a shade off kilter.

"Hello, please come in," she announced opening the door and directing me into the living room to the left of a short hall. I followed the worn trail in the beige wall-to-wall carpeting, and I took a seat on a long sofa with my back to the picture window. The room looked to have been last furnished in the nineties. Marge perched nervously on the edge of an occasional chair and stared at me as if expecting something. I smiled to put her at ease.

"I know who you are," she announced as if she had just solved a complex problem.

I resisted saying that I had called ahead, so she should know.

"I work at the library. They still talk about you there."

I nodded, a shade embarrassed. I didn't think I deserved to be seen as the tallest flower in the garden.

"It was something I did on impulse," I explained with a shrug.

"Not everyone would have done it."

"Everyone with the right training would have."

Marge shook her head. "You're being modest."

"No, only truthful. Now, why don't we talk about Joseph Teller?"

The smile left her face. "Poor Joe. You don't think he really committed suicide, do you?"

I took out my prop spiral notebook and placed it on my lap. I didn't want to begin with that question. I needed some background first.

"How did the two of you meet?"

"We met through a website for older people. He was such a gentleman, even when we just wrote back and forth, and he didn't disappoint when we met in person. He was very kind and gentle, but also very intelligent. He loved to talk about his earlier work in journalism, but he also listened to what I had to say. He was nothing like my ex-husband."

"What is he like?"

"He never wanted to talk. He would come in from work, complain about what he'd had to do all day, eat, and then go out to a bar. We never really talked about anything, if you know what I mean."

"The police mentioned to me that he'd been in trouble a few times."

"When he got a few beers in him, he'd be convinced that his opinion was the only right one and everybody had to accept it. If he happened to be sitting next to someone in the same condition who disagreed, they'd get into an argument. Owen was never slow to use his hands."

"Did he hit you?" I asked softly.

"No...never." She shook her head firmly. "He knew that if he did I would leave him."

"Why did you get divorced?" I was going well beyond the topic of my interview, but I suspected that she was willing to talk.

Marge smiled. "I got up one morning in the spring: the birds were singing, the sun was out. It was one of those days when you just feel everything is right with the world. Then I looked down at Owen, sleeping one off on the other side of the bed, and it spoiled my day. I realized that I was fifty-five years old and in good health, so I could have thousands more of those days where I would wake up happy and have it ruined by living with Owen. I just decided enough was enough."

"I imagine your husband was surprised."

"He couldn't believe it. He tried everything to get me to change my mind. He argued, he whined, he begged, he even threatened. But something had snapped inside me, and I couldn't have changed my mind even if I'd wanted to. The divorce was finalized in a year. I had a lot of the money I made over the years from my job that I never told Owen about, so when it came time for the settlement, I bought his share of the house. He's been renting over on the southwest side of town in a place near his favorite bar."

I folded my hands in my lap and gave her a long look. "I don't doubt what you're telling me, but your husband doesn't sound like the kind of guy who would give up easily."

She frowned and looked down at the worn carpeting. "He isn't. He would spy on me. I'd catch him at all hours driving past the house, and if he saw a strange car in front, he'd come up to the door and want to know what was going on. I suppose the police told you I finally got a restraining order."

"Is that how he got into a confrontation with Joe? Did he see his car parked in front of the house?"

"I suppose so. Joe had just brought me home from a date when there was a knock at the front door. It was Owen. 'What do you think you're doing?' he said to me. 'Having another man in my house.'"

"'It isn't your house anymore,' I told him. "And I can have any guest here that I like.'"

"What happened next?"

"Joe came over to see what was going on. I think Owen was a little frightened. He's a short guy and Joe was a lot taller. But that didn't stop him from telling Joe he'd better not see me again."

"Did they get into a fight?"

"No. But Owen did a lot of shouting and threatening. Then he stormed off and went back to his car. I'd had enough. The next day I went to the police and got a restraining order."

"What did Joe say?"

"Nothing much. He just chuckled when Owen left. I think he felt it was no big deal."

"Did Owen threaten to harm Joe?"

She gave me a penetrating look. "You don't think... I mean the police never suggested that anyone did this to Joe."

"The police haven't really formed a hypothesis."

"Well, Owen may have said that he would kill Joe if he saw him near me again, but Owen was always saying things like that. It may sound strange to say, but he wasn't strong enough to act on his threats."

"But he had been violent in the past?"

"That's true, but they were more drunken brawls. Things that he did on the spur of the moment when he'd had too much to drink."

"But what if he got jealous enough?"

Marge shrugged. "I guess Owen would do almost anything on impulse if the situation was right. I just can't see him attacking Joe in his office. That would require planning."

I nodded and changed gears. "Had Joe seemed depressed lately?"

"It was always hard to tell with Joe. He didn't talk a lot about his emotions. From what he said about his wife, I knew that he thought about her a lot, and sometimes he would look sad. But that's only natural, isn't it? And we had lots of fun together, so it wasn't like he was always talking about her and feeling down."

"So in your considered opinion, he wasn't suicidal?"

Marge twisted her hands and looked down at her lap. Tears came into her eyes. "No woman wants to feel that she wasn't making her boyfriend happy. I thought things were going well for us. When the police came around and started talking about suicide, I couldn't believe it."

"What do you think happened?"

"Like I told the police, I think it was just a terrible accident. Joe must have walked over to the window and had a dizzy spell or something. He was taking medicine for high blood pressure, you know."

"Did he mention getting dizzy?"

She shook her head. "But he wasn't the kind to complain about his health, unlike Owen who did nothing except whine about getting old from the time he was thirty."

"Did Joe mention anything about having problems at school?" I asked.

"Joe didn't talk about school much. He'd say a few general things now and then about the students not doing the work or about having a lot of papers to grade, but we never got into specifics." She paused for a moment. "You see, I never went to college, so it wasn't something that Joe and I had in common. Actually, it worried me a little. I thought my lack of education might divide us. I once mentioned it to Joe. I asked him if he felt there were a lot of things he couldn't talk to me about because I didn't have much education."

"What did he say?" I asked.

She smiled. "He said that I had more good sense than most people who went to graduate school, and he could talk to me about anything. He also said that it was more important that I was a nice person and a good cook."

That sounded a shade patronizing to me, but Teller probably had meant well.

"What sorts of things did you do together?"

Marge went on for some time about dinners out, attending the symphony in Springfield, going to museums in the area, and visiting historical sites. I dutifully made careful notes for my article.

When she was done, I stood up. "Thank you for your time. If your ex-husband gives you any more trouble, definitely let the police know. They'll take it seriously." I hoped that was true.

"I'm afraid I'm not seeing anyone right now, so there's nothing to get him upset," she said sadly.

"I'm sure you'll find someone else soon," I said, standing in the doorway.

"But nobody like Joe."

"Yes, special people aren't easily replaceable."

"Joe was certainly special. I just wish that I had met him sooner."

Chapter Thirteen

I drove back to my office. Once there, I decided it was time to set up an appointment with Rockwell Boyd. I called the English Department, and Janet Phillips told me that Professor Boyd had an office hour scheduled for four that afternoon.

"So I can just stop by and see him then?"

"Well, it is four on a Friday, so not many students are likely to show up, and frankly it's hard to know whether Professor Boyd will either. He sometimes comes in for the first ten minutes, and if no one shows, he goes home."

"I'll get there a few minutes before four, then, and hope for the best," I said.

"Yes, why don't you do that," she said, sounding pleased at the idea of forcing Boyd to keep his office hour.

Five minutes of four, I stood in front of Rockwell Boyd's office, looking down the hall with anticipation. I'd already walked from his office to Teller's. It was around a corner and about thirty yards away, so I doubted that Boyd would have heard a commotion in Teller's office if there had been one. I also calculated that Boyd's one window looked out on the front of the building rather than the side, so there was no way he had seen Joseph Teller fall, unless, of course, he was the one who had pushed him.

I heard him before I saw him. He was wearing boots with a high heel that clattered on the wooden floors and extended his height from about five-four to five-seven. He was in his mid-thirties, a trim, dapper fellow, wearing a form-fitting shirt and designer jeans. His right hand was full of mail he'd just picked up at the department office. His left hand clutched an expensive, tooled leather case. When he was a few feet away, he stopped dramatically and gave me a long glance, exaggerating how high his eyes had to travel.

"I know you're not one of my students," he said, smiling. "I'd remember you."

I was tempted to tell him that he'd drop from my memory in a second. Instead, I stuck out my hand. "I'm Kate Cameron, I'm doing a story for *The Sentinel* about Professor Teller."

"So you're a writer," he said, giving me a skeptical look.

"No, I'm actually a realtor, but I'm writing this article as a favor to the newspaper's editor."

"At least you're honest. So many people claim to be writers today that you'd think it was the easiest thing to do rather than one of the hardest."

He opened the door to his office and stepped inside. I followed. He took a seat behind his desk, which was covered with papers and exam books. I took a hard wooden chair obviously intended for students. On the floor was a rug of some complex oriental design. He saw me looking at it.

"A reporter friend got it out of Iran for me through the embargo," he said proudly. "It really is quite special."

I nodded and opened my notebook. "I was

wondering if you could tell me what you thought Professor Teller's contribution was to the department."

Boyd shrugged. "He taught journalism, I teach literature and creative writing. We really didn't have much in common, and due to our differing personalities and interests our paths didn't frequently intersect."

I feigned surprise. "You didn't like each other?"

"I wouldn't go that far. He was senior faculty, set in his ways and not very interested in younger faculty with new ideas. I'm sure he had been dynamic at one time in his life, probably when he was a working journalist. But like many people who leave an active career to teach about a field, I think he considered his position here to be a sort of semi-retirement."

"Yet many students over the last twenty years seem to have looked upon him as a mentor of sorts."

"Students striving to achieve a position in a profession tend to look upon anyone who's already reached that goal as a model. That doesn't mean that person has actually taught them very much beyond a few practical skills and an occasional amusing anecdote."

He picked up a clasp knife with a long blade and began slitting open his mail.

"That's quite a knife."

He nodded. "A mugger tried to use this on me once on the streets of Manhattan. I took it away from him."

Although I tried to conceal it, my doubts must have been reflected in my eyes.

"I may not look very tough," he said. "But I am actually quite agile and stronger than I appear. Also, when you see someone walking toward you with an attitude, you prepare for trouble. You should know about that."

I smiled. "Dean Messing has already spoken to you about me."

"Indeed, he warned me not to see you."

"But you went right ahead and did."

"I have nothing to hide."

"That's true of almost no one, and I know it isn't true of you."

"You're talking about my relationship with the dean. We are simply friends, and anyone who implies anything more had better be able to prove it."

"The mere accusation of favoritism would be enough to do both your careers considerable harm."

"No one would make such a charge."

"Even Professor Teller, if he felt he was being pressured to retire to make way for you?"

"Teller would never have brought that up in public. He had too much good taste and wouldn't have wanted to cause a scandal that would hurt the institution." Boyd smiled. "Sometimes having traditional values can hurt you."

"Maybe he'd have violated his principles. Desperate times lead to desperate measures."

Boyd frowned. "Is there anything else you'd like to ask me about Professor Teller?"

"You were here in your office at the time he died, were you not?"

"That's what they tell me. I have no idea when he died. I saw him go past my door heading down to his office. That's the last time I was aware of him."

"Did you see anyone else in the hall?"

"No, my office door was half-closed, and I was busy grading papers."

"So you neither heard nor saw anything unusual?"

"As I told the police, I didn't know that anything untoward had happened until the security guards began running down the hall shouting that someone had fallen from a window."

I looked across the office at a poster advertising an art exhibit.

"Professor Teller's death certainly opens up the door to your career aspirations, doesn't it?"

"What are you talking about?"

"All the tenured positions were filled, so there was really no place for you to go next year. You'd be eligible for tenure—perhaps even have earned it—but without a slot available the school would have had to let you go."

Boyd smiled confidently. It was a smile with charm spoiled by smugness. "I'm sure something could have been worked out."

"You think your friend, the dean, would have secured a position for you."

"I think my own talents would have guaranteed that the school didn't let me go."

I got to my feet. "It must be nice having that level of self-confidence."

"It's enabled me to achieve many things that would not otherwise have been possible. But I'm sure you're aware of the value of self-confidence. Without it, you'd have been dead on the floor of the library."

The image from my dream flashed before me, and I momentarily went cold.

"It was all a matter of training," I said.

He shook his head.

"Training is essential, but you have to have the

confidence to act on it at the right time." He smiled again. "So you see, we actually have quite a bit in common."

I turned and left his office.

Chapter Fourteen

I drove from the university to *The Sentinel* offices, brooding on Boyd's comment about our similarities. People had often commented on my self-confidence, which I generally considered to be a good thing. Timid people, in my experience, never accomplished very much, and I considered my willingness to make mistakes to be one of my better qualities, even if one that sometimes led to unfortunate results. But Boyd struck me as being more than merely confident; he had an arrogant quality that would allow him to run roughshod over others without a second thought. I could easily imagine him coming up with some plan to get rid of Teller if it were to his own benefit. But he seemed too clever—sneaky, actually—to push someone out a window to achieve his goal.

Myra was putting on her coat getting ready to leave as I walked in the door right on the dot of four. "She's already here. Been here about fifteen minutes," Myra said, rolling her eyes in the direction of the conference room. "I didn't want to leave them alone."

"Then I'd better get in there before they start locking lips," I whispered.

"Don't joke," Myra warned. "I know trouble when I see it, and that young woman is nothing but."

"Sorry, you could be right."

"I wish there were some way we could get rid of

her."

"I'm afraid Daniel doesn't see her as a problem."

Myra picked up her purse and headed for the door. "Men rarely do see a pretty woman as a problem—until it's too late."

I waved as she went out the door then walked into the conference room. Bianca was sitting to the right of Daniel as if to show that she was indispensable. He was poring over several pages of text, while she looked on with an expression of eager anticipation.

"What's going on?" I asked, trying to make the question sound non-accusatory.

Daniel glanced up and smiled. "Bianca has brought in a draft of the article the two of you are writing."

"Isn't that a bit premature?" I asked.

Bianca blushed. "I just wanted to get down all the background information we had in some kind of usable format. I figured we could always add whatever new material I discovered or you happened to find out."

"This is a good working draft," Daniel said, looking up at Bianca.

She smiled brightly and nodded. "Thanks. I hoped it would be useful." I could see that she wanted to reach out and touch his right hand. I wondered if she would have been able to resist if I hadn't been sitting there.

"Very much so," Daniel said. He turned to me. "I got a call from Detective Harrington a little earlier. He interviewed Dean Messing this afternoon. Apparently, he's got a solid alibi for the time of Joe Teller's death. He was in a meeting with the Administrative Council for the entire afternoon."

"Too bad. He certainly had a motive for wanting Teller gone," I said.

"It's never the one you suspect the most," Bianca said.

"Actually, it usually is," I replied tartly. "Only rarely is it hard to figure out who committed the crime. Criminals are generally pretty stupid. Proving it is the hard part."

Bianca shrugged as if nothing I said was worth considering.

"I also got a call from the dean yesterday," Daniel said. "He was complaining about your accusatory questioning. He seemed to feel *The Sentinel* was pursuing a vendetta against him."

"Well, I guess he's got nothing to worry about now," I said. "Although I can't say the same about his boyfriend Boyd. He had motive and opportunity. Harrington seemed to think he was too small to push Teller out a window, but the guy claims to have wrestled a knife away from a mugger. That makes him a possible in my book."

"Any other suspects?" Daniel asked.

I nodded. "Professor Teller had a girlfriend, Marge Rowen, and she had a jealous ex-husband with a record for assault. He might also be someone to consider."

"But from what I understand no one saw anyone in that hallway except for Boyd and Teller," said Daniel.

"It's worse than that. According to Harrington, the ex has an alibi. People say he was at work."

"So we're nowhere," Daniel moaned.

"Something will turn up," Bianca said brightly.

"Don't be so sure," I said. "Remember, it's still a possibility that Professor Teller took his own life."

"But he had a girlfriend and everything," Bianca said.

"Things aren't always that simple. Maybe he was struggling to start over but was just overcome by a wave of despair. It happens sometimes."

Bianca shook her head like it would never happen to her.

"Do we have anything else?" Daniel asked, tapping his pencil impatiently on the table.

One thing slowly surfaced in the back of my mind. "I talked to Professor Franks, the chair of the English Department, and she mentioned that Professor Teller was concerned about a possible plagiarism case with one of his students."

"If there was one thing Joe hated, it was plagiarism," Daniel said. "He often emphasized that it was the cardinal sin of journalism. You should always make sure that you investigate and cite all your sources."

"Do you know anything about a plagiarism case?" I asked Bianca.

She shook her head. "But I can ask my source."

"Are you willing to tell us who this person might be now?" I asked.

She got the standard stubborn pout on her face and shook her head.

I looked over at Daniel to see if he would lend some support to my request, but he just shrugged his shoulders. I felt helpless in the face of such childish petulance. If I were Daniel I would have threatened to fire her. That might have opened her up.

"But, be careful. We still don't know what this is all about," Daniel said to her.

Bianca beamed. "Don't worry. I can take care of myself."

Daniel adjourned the meeting. It took him several minutes of small talk to get Bianca to go. She was still clearly reluctant to leave her would-be boyfriend and me alone together. Finally, she got into her coat and left.

"I don't like her keeping this source a secret. She'd be safer if we both knew," I said.

"I'm not happy about it either, but it's probably another student, and you know how loyal and protective students can be with one another. Bianca probably sees us as the adult authorities, and giving us the name would be like turning in the person to the police."

"She doesn't see you as an adult authority."

He sighed. "Are we going to start on that again? I told you that I think you're all wrong about Bianca. She just looks up to me as a mentor, nothing more than that."

"Right."

He shrugged, his annoyance obvious. "Are we still on for tomorrow night?" he asked.

"Sure."

"Where do you want to go?"

"How about The River Bend Inn," I suggested. It was a nice restaurant just around the turn the river made from my condo. "I was imagining that we might go back to my place afterward."

Daniel's eyes lit up and he reached over and touched my shoulder. "It has been a while since we've had much private time together."

I nodded. Daniel's mother had been diagnosed with pneumonia a few weeks before so much of his spare time was tied up with nursing her. I guess you can't really pretend to have pneumonia and fool the doctor.

But I figured she was fully capable of it since her illness had begun right when Daniel began hinting around to her about the possibility of moving out of her house and getting a place of his own. He hadn't even broached the real issue of moving in with me. Who knew what illness that would cause?

"How about I pick you up around seven?" he said.

I nodded and gave him a kiss on the lips. After a moment he returned it with enthusiasm. I drove home looking forward to tomorrow night.

Chapter Fifteen

The next morning I bounded out of bed and went out for my morning run. I had to go to work this morning—it was my turn to cover the phones—but I still wanted to get in some exercise, so there was no time to lose. After showering and having a breakfast of juice, cereal, and coffee, I headed down the hill to the center of town. I figured I'd spend my time in the office checking out potential homes for the Hastings. The sooner I got rid of them the better.

I was alone in the office, deep into multiple listings, wondering how far I could push the Hastings' price point when the front door opened and my sister Amanda waltzed in. She walked over without a word and settled into one of my two client chairs.

"Good morning," I said cheerfully and got a curt nod in reply. "I'm surprised to see you here. How did you know where I was?"

"I drove by your place, and the car wasn't in the lot. So I figured you must be here."

"There are other places I might have been."

She gave me a scornful glance. "Where?"

I struggled to think of something that would enlarge the perimeter of my life. "I could have been shopping."

"You do that online."

She had me there. I've never been one to enjoy

shopping. "I could have been with a client."

"I know business has been slow lately. Of course, I suppose you might have been somewhere with Dave," Amanda said.

"That's Daniel," I corrected.

She smiled. She knew how to get my goat.

I leaned back in my chair and forced myself to stay calm. "So what brings you here on such a nice morning?"

"I wanted to apologize for being so bitchy to you the other night at dinner."

I stared at her. It wasn't like Amanda to apologize. Maybe she was growing up.

"This is where you jump in and say that I wasn't really bitchy, and you completely understand," she continued.

"You were, and I do."

She smiled. "Good, then everything is okay between us?"

"Never better."

"Then maybe you can help me. Dad is really putting the pressure on me to visit some four-year schools in the region. I need you to get him to back off."

"You insult me by suggesting that I have no life, then you ask for my help?"

"I was only kidding."

"Well, I think Mom and Dad are being generous. When I was graduating from high school, they pretty much told me that I had to go to Minton State or else get a basketball scholarship. Since I didn't want to play sports in college, that kind of narrowed my options to one."

"But you never wanted to go anywhere other than good old Minton State."

"As long as Mom and Dad were willing to let me live on campus, I was all right with it. If I'd actually had choices, however, who knows what I might have done? And George was given pretty much the same choice I was."

"He was happy anywhere he could study business and finance."

"I'm just telling you how it was. Neither of us had a choice."

"So now they have a lot of money left over because they deprived the two of you, and they want to spend it on me. Is that what you're saying?"

"Lucky you."

Amanda sighed. "Not really."

"Look, you've done better in high school than either George or I ever did. You're a whiz at math and science. They just want to see you develop your talents as far as possible. Why not take advantage of it?"

"Because I don't want to be cooped up behind a desk for the rest of my life like George or in front of a classroom like Dad. I want a more active life where things happen to me."

"In other words, you want to be a cop."

She nodded. "Is that so bad? After all, I got the impression that you enjoyed your time on the force—up until the end."

"Generally I did, I won't deny it. And I know what you mean about not wanting to sit around behind a desk for eight hours a day. One of the things I like about real estate is that I can pretty much make my own hours, and a lot of times I'm out at properties, not sitting in the office. But I wasn't kidding the other night. Pretty soon you will need a four-year degree to be a cop, or to get promoted anyway, and it's better to pick up the degree now than after you start working."

Amanda shrugged. "I'm tired of school. I think I can stand a couple of more years, but four seems like a total lifetime. After I've worked for a while, I'll probably feel more like going back."

"Mom doesn't want you to be a cop."

"She didn't want you to be one either."

"I know, but after what happened to me: first capturing that crazy shooter and then getting hit by the car, she's against it more than ever."

"Thanks for that," Amanda said sarcastically.

"It was no walk in the park for me either."

"Mom wants you to get married."

"For now she'll have to be satisfied with George being hitched."

"You and Daniel have no plans?"

"Let's just say our plans are very nebulous at the moment."

"Mom wants to know why I don't have a boyfriend."

"What happened to Tom?"

"That was Tim."

I gave her a gotcha smile, and she grinned. "We were just friends and did some things together. But he found someone to get more serious about."

"I'm sorry."

"Don't be." Amanda looked down at the floor and took a deep breath. "You know I'm gay, don't you?"

I caught my breath for a moment as well. "How *could* I know? You never told me. But I will admit I suspected. You're too cute not to have a bunch of guys hanging around unless for some reason you were strongly discouraging them."

She smiled. "Thanks, I think. Mom's got the idea that I keep guys away because I'm real serious about my studies. She says I should date and be more well rounded. Can you imagine? I can't come out to her, she would die."

"What about Dad?"

"I haven't told him, but I think, like you, he suspects. I figure he'd be pretty cool about it. After all, he's been hanging around high school kids most of his life. Mom is the one I worry about."

"She might surprise you. I don't think she's quite as traditional as she pretends to be. After all, she was a surgical nurse for a lot of years up until you came along, and she had three kids to take care of. She's had her own ambitions and probably met a lot of different people."

"I guess."

"You'll have to tell them eventually."

"In my own good time—okay?"

I nodded. "Is that why you want to leave school as soon as possible because you don't think you'll fit in?"

"I suppose that's part of it."

"Well, it won't be any easier on a police force. The guys are okay, but most of them are pretty conservative. And you're always going to attract a lot of male attention. It's going to be hard to hide your preferences."

"I wish I looked more like you."

"Thanks a lot."

She smiled. "No, I mean more athletic and less

well endowed. Then maybe guys would leave me alone."

"Dream on. You could be flat as a plank and ugly as a hoe, and some guys would still be interested."

Amanda laughed. "I suppose you're right."

I paused and stared at the screen saver on my computer. It showed a white colonial with a picket fence and an expanse of green lawn: the American dream for the perfect American family. Even in Minton, things were changing.

"Do you have a girlfriend?" I asked.

She blushed. "There is someone, but I'm not ready to talk about it yet."

"No problem. That's your business. But to get back to the original matter, I think you should reconsider hurrying to leave school. Being four years older will make you more mature. You'll be surer of what you want to do and more confident about the kind of person you want to be. A college or university is a lot better place to find out about that stuff than a local police force."

Amanda paused for a long moment, hopefully considering my advice. Finally, she smiled. "Thanks, sis," she said. Something she never calls me. "Believe it or not, some of what you said might actually be useful."

"Happy to be of help."

"And remember, this was just between us. Nothing goes any further."

"On my oath as a realtor."

Amanda smirked and left the office. I sat behind my desk and spun around slowly in my ergonomic chair thinking how little we understand people's reasons for what they do. That just brought me back to thinking about Daniel and Bianca. I wondered if perhaps I shouldn't have turned the tables and asked Amanda for a little advice about my own love life.

Chapter Sixteen

I had just gotten back to my multiple listings; trying hard to concentrate on the Hastings after the news Amanda had given me when my cell phone rang.

"This is Daniel."

I could tell he was upset because he always identified himself when something had gone wrong as if wanting to be certain that I knew who was speaking.

"What's the matter?"

"I just got a call from Detective Harrington. Bianca was attacked and injured on campus last night."

I could hear the anxiety in his voice and immediately switched into police mode. "What do the cops know so far?"

"Not much. A student out for her morning run found her early this morning unconscious under a tree. It's a dark part of the campus, a wooded area. The police think she was heading out to the parking lot, getting her car to drive to class when she was attacked. It could have been an attempted rape or a mugging. Her cell phone and money were missing."

"Is she going to be all right?"

"No one seems to know. I guess she suffered a nasty blow to the head. She's in the intensive care unit at the hospital."

"Right here in town?"

"Yeah."

Minton has a small hospital. It's named Walthrop Hospital after an early settler of the town. It was now affiliated with a bigger medical center in Springfield, but it still offered a range of services. I thought it was a good sign that Bianca hadn't yet been transferred to the larger facility.

"Harrington wanted to know if Bianca had been involved in our investigation into the Teller case," Daniel said.

"What did you tell him?" I asked.

"The truth. I said that she had been asking around campus to see if anyone knew anything about Teller's death."

"Did you mention that she had a secret source?"

"Yes. He seemed pretty annoyed that I hadn't kept closer track of whom she was speaking to." Daniel sighed. "Actually he was angry that I'd gotten a student involved in the investigation at all."

I imagined Daniel was downplaying the level of Harrington's response. Police never like civilian involvement in investigations, and here we had a person below the age of twenty-one getting seriously injured while playing cop. That was a police nightmare. I was certain he had been furious and let Daniel know.

"You were right," Daniel said.

"About what?"

"I gave her too much leeway. I allowed her enthusiasm—and, I guess, her flattery—to blind me to the fact that she's only a kid and shouldn't be allowed to work without strict supervision. I don't know what I thought I was doing, letting her investigate what could be a murder."

Finally, the light had dawned. I hoped it wasn't too

late for Bianca. "If there is a connection between the attack on Bianca and the Teller case, this proves that Teller most certainly was murdered. Has she been able to tell the police anything about who did it?"

"According to Harrington she hasn't regained consciousness yet, so they haven't been able to question her."

That didn't sound good. If she was in a prolonged coma, there might be the possibility of permanent brain damage.

Daniel cleared his throat. It was a harsh sound, and I pulled the phone back from my ear.

"Look, I want to go over to the hospital. I was wondering if you'd be willing to go with me."

"They won't let you see her if she's in the ICU. You aren't family."

"I have some contacts at the hospital. Maybe I'll be able to get in."

"To what purpose? She's unconscious."

"I just want to see her," he said, his voice rising. "Don't you understand? I feel responsible."

I bit back my response that feeling guilty was no excuse for doing stupid things. He was in no condition to be argued with.

"Of course, I'll go with you. When do you want to meet?"

"Fifteen minutes."

"I have to cover the phones here for another half an hour. I can meet you after that."

"I'm going over there now," he said, in a stubborn, betrayed tone. "Meet me at the ICU whenever you can get there."

The phone went dead. I got the distinct impression

that he had expected me to instantly drop everything to go gaze at Bianca's unconscious figure. That he felt the need to do that worried me. It indicated that his attachment to the girl might be stronger than I had thought. I wondered if Daniel was the kind of man who needed a woman to be dependent on him. Maybe that explained his close relationship to his needy mother and to a girl over a decade younger. If that was what Daniel was looking for, he was probably sorely disappointed in me. I was more into a partnership of equals than dependency. I wondered whether Daniel had failed to pressure his mother more on the issue of our living together because he sensed that ultimately it wouldn't work out.

My mind quickly scooted back over a series of half-forgotten instances where we had rubbed each other the wrong way because Daniel wanted to do something and I'd resisted going along. I knew I wasn't the most accommodating of people, but I was pretty good at cobbling together compromises without getting distraught. Daniel, on the other hand, seemed to invest more emotion in getting his own way.

I was still pursuing that grim line of thought when Molly came in half an hour later to relieve me. I quickly left and drove over to the hospital about a mile away.

Through the glass wall of intensive care, I could see about fifteen beds arranged around the room, and several nurses staffing a desk by the front door. Monitors hung from the ceiling in front of them, which they seemed to check regularly. I looked around the lobby and spotted Daniel slumped on a bench in a corner.

"Can't get in?" I asked.

He shook his head. "They only let in two people at a time, and Bianca's parents are with her now. There's some good news. She's regained consciousness."

"That's great."

I heard the *swoosh* of the sliding doors opening behind me. I turned and saw a middle-aged couple come out of intensive care. The woman saw us and started in our direction. The man seized her arm and tried to pull her down a side hall, but she violently shrugged off his hand. She marched toward us, her face stiff with anger.

"Are you Daniel Rencardi?" she asked, staring hard at him.

He climbed to his feet. "I am. Mrs. Fitzsimmons, let me tell you how sorry…"

"Be quiet. There's nothing you can tell me that will make the slightest bit of difference. My little girl is lying in there right now and may never be the same, and it's your fault. It was always 'Daniel this and Daniel that.' She thought you walked on air. I knew it wasn't healthy her having a crush on an older man like that. But what could I do, you can't talk to a girl that age. I could only hope you would behave yourself."

Daniel blushed. "I assure you…"

"I don't mean that. I just hoped you would have the good sense to rein in her enthusiasm. But no, instead you let her get involved in investigating a murder."

"I didn't know it was a murder."

"But you suspected. I've already had a conversation with the police, and I have a pretty good idea what was going on." She turned to stare at me. "You and your girlfriend here used my daughter to get information from students. Didn't it ever occur to you

110

that she might be in danger?"

"We're sorry about what happened," I said calmly. I'd long ago learned that responding to emotion with emotion never paid off.

She ignored me and turned her attention back to Daniel. "And let me assure you that if Bianca doesn't make a complete recovery—and I mean complete—I plan to sue you personally and the newspaper you work for. So help me, you'll regret the day you used my daughter to get a good story."

"Let's go now, Chris," her husband said, gently taking her arm.

"And when I come back, I don't want to see either one of you here. I don't want you trying to see my daughter, and if you won't leave, I'll call the police and file charges."

Giving us one more backward glance, she let herself be led away down the hall by her husband who gave us a somber look. I had a feeling that, if anything, his emotions ran deeper than his wife's. My experience on the job was that the person who expresses his or her emotions is often less dangerous than the one who lets them silently simmer.

"Let's get out of here," I said, taking Daniel's arm and pulling him down another hallway from the one Bianca's parents had entered.

"I still want to see her, especially if she's conscious," Daniel insisted, turning back.

"That's not possible, and even if it were, it wouldn't be wise."

"I don't care about getting sued."

"Yes, you do. You may not realize it right now but you do. It would ruin your life. Stay out of this, and you may get away with only having a guilty conscience."

His head hung down as though he expected to be struck. "Don't you think I deserve more than that?"

"You were naïve and underestimated the obsession of a young woman. That was foolish but not malicious. You don't deserve to be punished. Let's save that for the real culprit, whoever attacked Bianca."

I started walking down the hall. After a moment he caught up to me.

"How are we going to find out who did this to Bianca?"

"If it is connected to what she was doing for us, then we keep doing what we intended to do: find out what happened to Professor Teller."

"Can we accomplish that?"

"You mean without Bianca? I think so. Somebody on campus must know whom she was talking to, and if I ask around enough, I might be able to find out. Plus I'd like to come up with a way to put more pressure on Professor Boyd. I still see him as our primary suspect."

Daniel stopped and turned to face me. "Thank you, Kate, for being willing to carry on with this investigation. I appreciate it. I know you didn't really want to get involved in the whole thing in the first place."

"I didn't. However, now that I am, I'm as anxious as you are to solve it."

"First Joe Teller, now Bianca, this is getting personal to me."

"Save that passion for when we write the story. Let me be the professional in the investigation, the one who isn't emotionally involved. In other words, don't go off investigating on your own. Okay?"

He nodded.

"Are we still on for dinner tonight?"

"I'd better not. I told my mother about Bianca when I got the call at home, and she was pretty upset. I'd better spend the evening with her."

"Fine. We'll reschedule for another time soon," I said, hiding my disappointment. It seemed to me that I had been doing that a lot lately.

We walked side by side back to the entrance to the hospital. During that brief walk, I began to seriously wonder if we'd be walking side by side very much longer.

Chapter Seventeen

The next day was Sunday. I'd spent Saturday night brooding on what might have been and trying to trace my way back to where things had started to go wrong between Daniel and myself. One of the problems with having an analytical mind is that I obsess over my own actions even when it was unlikely to do any good. If it was over between Daniel and me, what difference did it make to detail the gradual disintegration of the relationship? It probably wouldn't help me with my next boyfriend. After all, each pairing was unique. Finally, I decided that deep down I was looking for a way to repair what we had between us because I really liked Daniel and hated to have us split up. As much as I felt that way, however, instead of seeing Daniel through the windshield as my future, I was increasingly spotting him in my rearview mirror as part of my past.

I spent Sunday morning cleaning the condo. I always clean on Sundays. If I don't keep to a schedule, it just didn't get done, and I hated living in dirt and clutter. But this morning, I really went overboard, moving the sofa to vacuum the rug, steaming the tile in the kitchen and baths, and wiping down all the cabinetry. By lunchtime I was exhausted but able to take a quiet pride in what I had accomplished, proving to myself that I was perfectly capable of living alone. I figured that given my track record with men I'd better get used to it. Judging by the disorder Daniel tolerated in the newsroom, I had a suspicion that this was another point we would have clashed on.

I had an early lunch because I was scheduled to cover an open house from one until three in the afternoon. The place belonged to an older couple that was planning to move into senior housing. It was filled with artifacts going back to the early years of their marriage, and they had a basement chock-a-block with stuff, most of which belonged to their three children who stubbornly refused to come and claim it. I kept urging them to minimize what they had in the upstairs rooms so it would appear more spacious, and potential buyers could better visualize the house as their own. I even gave them the name of a friend of mine who specialized in emptying out houses that were for sale, selling what was valuable and disposing of the rest. But so far they had resisted, giving me helpless shrugs, as if the dimension of the task was simply overwhelming them. I had a feeling that they were not truly convinced that their house would ever sell and that getting an actual buyer would galvanize them into action.

I got dressed in my usual open house outfit of blouse, slacks, and sports jacket. I wore the jacket so it would conceal the waistband holster where I carried my Glock. A lot of retired cops still carry their firearms all the time, partly because they don't want to admit that they're no longer on the job and partly out of a desire to continue protecting the public. I almost never carry a weapon. I had no trouble leaving the job—or at least that's what I told myself—and I doubted that Minton would be much safer if I went around armed. However, open houses were another matter. National statistics showed that female realtors were in considerable danger waiting around alone to meet strangers in empty houses, especially those in rural areas. I had no intention of becoming a victim, so I carried.

I took my signs out of the spare bedroom that doubles as storage and a guest room and put them in the trunk of my car. I returned upstairs and got my big bag that contained the flyers describing the house, then I headed out. I stopped several times along the route to post a sign guiding people to the open house, which was in a small development across the street from a still active cornfield. When I got to the house I saw that since my last visit the cornfield had been reduced to stubble, I put my last sign at the end of the driveway, so even the directionally impaired couldn't get lost.

I rang the bell, but fortunately, no one was home. I always hate it when the owners stay around to give you last minute directions on how to do your job or, worse yet, want to meet the visitors to point out all the unique and wonderful attributes of their home. All this does is prevent potential buyers from imagining the house as their own. I opened a couple of windows because the house was kind of stuffy and placed my handouts on the kitchen counter. Then I waited for the crowd to rush in.

It was more a trickle than a cascade. Three couples came in during the first hour. They toured the house and left without much comment, aside from one woman mentioning that the place could use some updating. I pointed out to her that at its asking price the house was a bargain and would leave a buyer with plenty of money for changes. She listened politely but clearly remained unconvinced.

During the second hour, a man came in alone. I

kept a wary eye on him until he admitted that he was from the neighborhood and had always wanted to see what the inside of the house was like. He was wasting my time, but not a threat. Two more couples wandered through, but they seemed more as though they were out for an afternoon jaunt on a pleasant fall day than seriously in the market for a home. On the stroke of two, I packed my bag, locked the door, and walked down the driveway to get my sign. I was about to pick it up when I heard the crack of gunfire, and my sign went flying off onto the front lawn. I dropped my bag and spun around, pulling my Glock from its holster. Across the way in the middle of the cornfield, I saw a short, thin man stand up carrying a rifle and begin running toward the next road over like an armed scarecrow who had just realized the growing season was over.

I put my gun back in the holster, deciding that this had become a foot race. There was no way I was going to go charging through a stubble-strewn field in my good shoes, so I took off running up the street. I could see the pickup truck the guy was heading for parked along a road that ran perpendicular to the one I was on. By cutting off the angle, he had the advantage of distance, but by the way he was already staggering across the field, I figured I had the benefit of speed.

I'm not as fast as I was in high school by any means, but even without the right equipment, I was way faster than the guy I was chasing. He was bent over in pain and stumbling by the time he reached the side of his truck, and I was closing in fast. Fifteen more feet and I would have caught him. As it was, he pulled away with a belch of smoke, just before I could grab his tailgate, which wouldn't have done me much good. But as I watched him drive up the street, I carefully wrote down his plate number in the palm of my hand. Never rely on your memory when you have an alternative.

The cop who responded to my call was someone I knew casually from my time on the force. We recognized each other and nodded, each agreeing to leave past awkwardness unmentioned. He listened to what I had to say, took a long look at the bullet hole in the sign, and wrote down the plate number I recited to him. He returned to his car where I assumed he was firing up his computer. In a few minutes, he returned at his usual regulation saunter.

"Do you know an Owen Dragmore?"

"I don't know him. But I do know that he's a person of interest in a case the Detective Harrington is investigating."

I saw a calculating flash of brightness in his eyes as he saw an opportunity to ingratiate himself with Harrington. I knew he was dying of curiosity and very much wanted to ask me what the case was about, but that would mean requesting information from a civilian—a sure sign of weakness.

"I'll take care of it," he said, clearly implying that I shouldn't worry my pretty little head about it any further.

I smiled demurely and thanked him for responding. I figured that if I didn't hear from Harrington in a couple of hours, I'd call him myself.

I drove home wondering why Dragmore had taken a shot at me. I figured it was more to scare than to injure. Given the distance, he either hadn't wanted to hit me or was an incredibly bad shot. Of course, there was always the possibility that he'd been visiting his local bar before arriving on the scene which meant that my escape had been due more to luck than planning. That thought sent a cold shiver up my spine.

The other question that occurred to me was how had Dragmore found out about me in the first place? The more I thought about it, the more I realized there was only one answer.

Chapter Eighteen

As soon as I got home, I pulled out my cell phone and called Marge Rowen. She seemed happy to hear from me and anxious to talk. I imagined that living alone might make the days drag.

"I was just wondering, have you been in contact with your ex-husband recently?" I asked when there was finally a break in her chatter.

There was a long pause. "As a matter of fact, I spoke to him yesterday on the phone."

"Did you happen to mention my name?"

"I'm afraid I did. I hope I didn't do anything wrong. He hasn't been threatening you, has he?"

"Not exactly." That was true; he'd skipped right over the threat stage. "What did you tell him?"

"Well, I told him you were going to write a piece for *The Sentinel* about what a fine man Joseph was. That seemed to get Owen very angry. He said that I should forget about Joe and that there was no man for me but him. I told him not to be foolish. We were over and things were never going back to the way they were."

She said this all in such a calm, reasonable voice that I imagined it would drive a volatile guy like Dragmore crazy. "Did you say anything about my investigating Joe's death?"

"I may have mentioned it," she admitted

reluctantly.

This must have been a more extensive conversation than Marge cared to admit. I wondered about her willingness to have lengthy conversations with her husband. Was she really as over him as she professed?

"You know, I was actually about to give you a call myself," Marge said. "You asked me whether Joseph had ever talked at all about things at school."

"And you said he didn't, at least not very often."

"Right. But then I remembered that the weekend before Joe died, we had lunch together in a little restaurant up in Northampton. We'd been up to see the fall flowers at the Smith College Arboretum and decided on a whim to stay for lunch."

"I see."

"Well, we were seated in a corner behind a half-wall, where we could see the rest of the room, but they couldn't see us. Joseph was looking at the other people when I saw his eyes widen, and I asked him what was wrong."

"And what did he say?" Marge could certainly string out a story for drama.

"He told me that one of the two men at the table by the window was Rockwell Boyd, a professor in the English Department. I looked over and saw two men sitting there holding hands across the table, like they were more than friends, if you know what I mean?"

"And one of them was Rockwell Boyd?"

"According to Joe, it was the one sitting with his back to me."

"Did Joseph mention who the other one was?"

"He said he didn't know him. He was a handsome man in his early thirties."

So Boyd was cheating on Messing. The dean might have been a lot of things, but he would never be mistaken for a handsome man in his early thirties.

"I don't think Professor Boyd was happy that we saw him having lunch with that man."

"How do you know?"

"He and the other man finished their lunch first. As they were walking out, he looked over and saw Joe and me. Joe nodded at him. Boyd came to a dead stop and just stared. I know it's probably an exaggeration, but he actually seemed to turn pale like they say in books. I would say that the man was positively frightened at seeing us there."

"Did Joe say anything?"

"No, he may have smiled a little to himself, but that's all. I asked him why the man seemed so upset, but Joe didn't tell me."

I knew the answer to that. Having the person you were trying to force out of his job know that you were cheating on the dean, your major supporter, would no doubt take your breath away. Boyd might well have figured that if he pursued his plans to get him ousted, Teller would inform the dean of his boyfriend on the side. That would pretty much guarantee that Boyd would be looking for another job next year. It also provided a pretty good motive for murder.

I thanked Marge, not telling her about Dragmore using me for target practice. There was no sense in upsetting her without reason. Harrington called me about an hour later.

"Can you positively identify Owen Dragmore as the shooter?"

"Not exactly. I've never met him. But he fit the

description Marge gave me of her ex, and he was driving his truck."

"If I pulled him in, would you be able to identify him? Did you get a good look at his face?"

I thought of the moment when the man reached the truck and pulled open the door. For an instant, he turned to face me, and I was only a few feet away.

"I can identify him."

"Good. We'll bring him in. Do you have any idea why he would take a shot at you?" asked Harrington.

"His wife told him about the story on Teller I was writing. I think he's got an irrational hatred for the man and doesn't want to see him get positive publicity. He also may not be happy about my investigating the case."

"Especially if he was the one who killed Teller."

"That's a bit of a leap, but it's worth considering."

"It certainly is."

"By the way, I just had a conversation with Marge Rowan," I said, and went on to tell him about Teller seeing Boyd with a different friend.

"That would put the cat among the pigeons," Harrington said. "If Teller threatened to tell Messing, Boyd might have been motivated to kill him."

"Another reason to focus attention on the professor."

"Right. I'll give you a call once we've got Dragmore."

I changed into my casual clothes and got dinner started. Then I sat down with a glass of wine and thought about the day. Only then did my hand begin to shake so much that I set the wine down on the end table to keep it from spilling. I'd been inches away from being hit by a bullet, which, even if it didn't kill me, could have smashed my spine and changed my life forever. I've always been that way. I can function fine in times of danger, but afterward, once I have a chance to reflect, the full impact hits me.

I wondered if I had just added another nightmare to my list.

Chapter Nineteen

Fiona Halsey was all by herself in the English Department office when I arrived the next morning. She stood behind her desk, keeping it between us as if for protection. She stared at me through her thick glasses and squared her broad shoulders as if readying herself for another barrage of questions.

"You remember me from the other day, don't you? I work for *The Sentinel*, and I'm doing a story on Professor Teller."

"I remember you," she said sharply as if it wasn't an all-together pleasant memory.

"Did you also know that Bianca Fitzsimmons was also working on the same story? You probably know her, she's an English major."

"I know Bianca, and pretty much everyone knows that she works for *The Sentinel*."

I got the feeling that Bianca probably bragged a bit about her job in journalism.

"Did you also hear that she was attacked on campus Friday night?" I asked.

Fiona nodded. "That was terrible. I went to the next dorm to do my laundry last night, and I was looking over my shoulder the whole time."

"Do you know if Bianca had any enemies who would want to hurt her?"

Fiona's eyes opened wider behind her glasses.

"You mean you think someone *she knew* did this? I figured it was just some pervert attacking a random girl."

"Well, of course, it could be," I said in a soothing voice. She looked to be on the edge of panic. "I was just wondering if anyone came to mind."

"I don't know Bianca all that well. We're both English majors, so I saw her in some literature classes. But I'm not a journalism minor like she is." Fiona paused for a moment. "How is Bianca? What does she say happened?"

"Well, she has regained consciousness, but I don't know what she's been able to tell the police."

"I hope she can identify whoever did this. We don't need people like that on campus."

I nodded and changed the subject. "Have you heard anything about a case of student plagiarism that Professor Teller was concerned about?"

"No. But the faculty would never talk to me about that since I'm only a student." She gave me a level glance. "And even if I did know, I couldn't talk to you about it because it would be a confidential department matter."

I could see that the English Department had made a good choice in student interns at least when it came to discretion. "I was just wondering…"

There were footsteps behind me, and Fiona glanced over my shoulder with relief written on her face. I turned around and saw Janet Phillips looking at me sternly.

"Can I help you?" she asked.

"I was just asking Fiona if she knew anyone who would have wanted to hurt Bianca."

Janet Phillips turned and motioned for me to follow her out into the hall. She walked several feet away from the open door and faced me.

"I don't want you getting Fiona all upset. She's a very fragile girl. She's an excellent student, but her social skills are weak, and she's easily disturbed by harsh people."

I smiled. "I certainly didn't mean to be harsh."

"I didn't say you did, not objectively that is. But some students can be very upset just by the wrong tone of voice. We forget that although they appear to be adults in many ways, they are still children."

"Thank you for warning me. I'll keep that in mind. But you have to understand I am naturally very concerned about what happened to Bianca. She was a colleague of mine." The words weren't easy to say, but in a sense, they were true. "I was simply trying to find out if she had any enemies who would have wanted to hurt her."

"Surely this was a random attack."

I sighed. I'd been down this road before. "Possibly, but Bianca was working on an article about Professor Teller. She was questioning people, and I'm wondering if she spoke to the wrong person."

Janet looked puzzled. "What are you trying to say? Wasn't Professor Teller's death a suicide?"

"That's one hypothesis."

"But surely you don't think someone pushed him from that window?"

"That's another thought."

She shook her head. "I find that very hard to believe. This is a university; people here don't act like a bunch of ruffians. Professor Teller's death is certainly tragic, but I'm certain it didn't involve foul play."

"What about Bianca? Did she have enemies?"

Janet Phillips smiled. "Bianca was the exception that proved the rule when it comes to students being adults. She was definitely a very mature young woman and absolutely fearless. I've only heard rumors, but she's apparently confronted boys accused of assaulting girls and tried to interview them. She's also approached drug dealers on campus, faculty accused of discriminating against women, and students caught cheating. I don't know if many of her efforts have resulted in published articles, although she did have a piece in *The Sentinel* last year about the use of school funds to finance faculty dinners. That got a few administrators riled up at her."

"Dean Messing?"

Janet smiled. "I believe he was mentioned in the story."

"How about more recently? Do you know if she's approached anyone in the last few days who may have become angry with her?"

"Not that I've heard about. But not every event makes its way into the staff rumor mill. And I'd have thought it more likely that some irate administrator would try to get her expelled rather than hit her over the head."

"Perhaps her conflict was with another student."

"That I'd be less likely to know about."

I looked down the dark shadowy hall and breathed in deeply the smell of old wood and floor polish.

"Speaking of student issues, were you aware that Professor Teller thought one of his students had plagiarized a paper?"

"No, but under most circumstances, I wouldn't be informed; that would be handled by the department chair, the faculty member, and possibly the dean if expulsion was involved. Only if the student filed a formal protest to the Faculty Student Rules committee would anyone else become aware of it."

"So you have no idea who the student is whose work was being called into question by Professor Teller?"

"Not at all. And he was teaching four sections this semester: two of journalism and two of technical writing. That means he had almost a hundred students, and knowing Professor Teller, they've all had to hand in several written assignments already. It would be very hard to narrow it down."

I paused as an idea came to me. "Is Professor Teller's office still the way it was at the time of his death?"

"Yes. The police sealed it off and asked us to keep everyone out until further notice."

"So it's been locked. Who has the key?"

"I have a master key to all the offices and Professor Franks has one. But I can't let you in without police permission."

I smiled at her in what I hoped wasn't a harsh way.

"I wouldn't dream of it," I replied.

Chapter Twenty

My cell phone rang right after I got settled behind my desk back at work. It was Daniel.

"Bianca is out of intensive care and in a private room," he announced.

"That's good news."

"She wants to see me."

"That would be a very bad idea."

"Her parents aren't coming to visit her in the morning, so we could do it without them ever knowing."

"Unless Bianca tells them in some fit of youthful defiance. I don't think her mother was bluffing about her threat to sue. If she even hears we've been in to see her daughter, you could find yourself in court."

There was a long pause. "We have to discover who attacked Bianca. That could be the answer to the Teller case."

"Let the police question her. I'm sure Detective Harrington will let me know what he finds out."

"I'd like you to go with me," Daniel said, skipping over my objections like they hadn't been spoken. "I think it would be more...proper."

Now he was suddenly worried about propriety. "Okay, I'll come with you. But I want to be on record that I don't think we should do this."

"Fine. Can you make it to the hospital in half an

hour?"

I said I could. Afterward, I sat there staring out the window at the town green. A few people were hurrying across either on their way to the library or to one of the shops that bordered the street circling around it. It was a typical Monday morning in Minton. I tried to relax into the scene, but I kept wondering whether Daniel's desire to see Bianca was really based on his wish to solve the Teller case or whether he had a more personal interest in seeing her. I also didn't like having my advice summarily ignored. It made me feel that I didn't count for anything in his life. He was either so obsessed with Bianca or so sure of his own rightness that he wouldn't even consider my warnings. Once again I felt that our time together was coming to an end.

A half hour later I met Daniel in the lobby of the hospital. He had just gotten her room number from the woman at the switchboard. We took an elevator up to the third floor and walked down a corridor to our right.

"Did she say how she was when you talked to her on the phone?"

"I asked, but she said she'd tell me when I came to visit."

Typical young drama queen, I thought, stretching out the reveal to the last possible moment.

"The next room is hers," Daniel said; ready to walk through the door.

I grabbed his arm and held him back. I peeked around the corner to make sure her parents weren't there. I wouldn't put it past Bianca to stage a confrontation for some obscure purpose of her own. The room was empty. There was a bed in which a figure lay with her eyes closed.

We went inside. As we approached the bed, I was surprised at how small Bianca looked under the covers. She really was very petite, not making much of a lump under the blanket. Her eyes were closed, either because she didn't realize we were there or she was feigning sleep. Her head was wrapped in a white turban of bandages that made her look vaguely foreign, and with her hair covered, she had an oddly asexual appearance as if she could be a girl or a pretty young boy. She opened her eyes and saw Daniel. Her face broke into a broad smile. Then she saw me.

"What's *she* doing here?"

Daniel appeared taken aback by the question and didn't answer.

"In case you don't remember," I said, "we're colleagues. We're working together on the story of Joseph Teller's death."

"We're not colleagues. You're a real estate agent, not a journalist."

"And you're a college student who has gotten herself in over her head," I replied. "Do you have any idea who attacked you?"

"No," she said, putting on one of her patented petulant expressions.

"Maybe you could tell us what you do remember from that night?" Daniel asked in a gentle voice.

Bianca sighed. "I left my dorm and was walking to the parking lot where I keep my car. I have a night class across campus two nights a week, so I always drive over there. I was walking on the path under the trees. It's kind of spooky there, so I was walking pretty fast. All of a sudden I heard footsteps behind me. I started to turn around to see who it was when something hit me.

That's all I remember until I woke up here in the hospital."

"Did you get a look at the person who hit you?" I asked.

"No," she said quickly, not really considering my question.

"Do you have any idea of their size or gender? Anything at all would be helpful," Daniel said with an encouraging smile.

Bianca returned his smile and relented. "The person was taller than I was, really just a dark figure. That's all I could see before my vision went black."

Since about ninety-percent of the adult population was taller than Bianca, I didn't think it was very valuable information.

"How about telling us the name of your contact? That will help us follow up on the investigation," I said.

"I can't remember. I really can't remember much about what I did for the last couple of days."

"But you remember me."

She glared as if I was someone she'd never forget. "The doctor said it was probably temporary selective amnesia. I remember some things but not others. Eventually, it should all come back if I'm lucky. It's not that unusual when someone has suffered a blow to the head."

I knew what she said was correct, and the condition wasn't that uncommon. I remembered a situation I'd handled once when a young woman in an auto accident didn't recognize her own family for several days after the event. In Bianca's case, however, I wouldn't put it past her to lie just to prevent us from solving the case without her help. I glanced over at Daniel. He was looking at her sympathetically. I wondered whether he was just gullible or in love.

"I have a problem," she said slowly, staring soulfully at Daniel as if he could easily solve all her problems. "I'm afraid my parents are insisting that I quit the newspaper. They think that this happened to me because I was involved in the Teller case. I tried to tell them that this sort of stuff happens on campuses all the time, and it probably had nothing to do with my work on the story. But they don't believe me. They said that if I don't leave *The Sentinel* they wouldn't continue to pay my tuition."

Daniel shook his head at the unreasonableness of it all. I had thought we agreed that the Teller case probably was related to the attack on Bianca, but here was Daniel being sucked back into her dubious version of events. I knew what was coming next.

Bianca gazed into Daniel's eyes. "I thought that maybe you could convince my parents that I have a real future as a journalist, and this is my best opportunity to get some credibility while still in college."

"I'd like to help you," Daniel said, "but I really don't think your parents are going to listen to me. They blame me for what happened to you."

"We shouldn't be here right now," I said. "If your parents find out about it, they will probably sue Daniel. It could cost him his job."

Bianca smiled smugly. "They really wouldn't do that. I wouldn't let them."

I felt a surge of anger at her infuriating complacency. "I don't think you have any idea how determined frightened parents can be. They will sue Daniel, and they will pull you out of school if you don't stop working on *The Sentinel.*"

"I'm not going to give up my chance to be a journalist."

"And you shouldn't," I said more softly. "From everything I've heard around campus you are a fearless person who will confront anyone for a story. That's a fine thing, and with your looks, you may even have a career in television news. But this is a time to back away before you destroy your chances and Daniel's."

My compliment seemed to surprise her, and she actually stopped for a minute to think. A crafty expression came over her face. "Do you really think I might have a chance in the media?" she asked me.

I nodded and saw my opening. "I bet you'd have a good on-camera presence, and let's face it, print journalism is struggling to stay alive. There are very few jobs. Your chances are much better on television."

"I'm only a junior," she said thoughtfully. "I still have time to pick up a communications minor."

"Sure you do. That would be a smart move."

I smiled to myself. Clearly, Bianca was someone who was most easily swayed by self-interest.

She gave Daniel a lingering look like he was already a part of her past, cataloged in her album of might-have-beens.

"I'm sorry," she said, "but I think I'd better listen to my parents. I certainly can't afford to leave college right now, and I wouldn't want them to do anything to hurt you."

Daniel nodded, appearing dazed at the sudden turn of events. "When you get out of the hospital come by and pick up your last check," he said, getting to his feet a little shakily.

"Don't worry," she said with a bright smile. "I'll stop in to say goodbye."

"Good luck to you," I said.

"I hope you can handle the Teller story without me."

"I'll do my best," I assured her.

Daniel turned to me as we walked down the hall from Bianca's room.

"What just happened there?" he asked.

"You just learned about the fickleness of a young girl's heart."

Daniel grunted. "I told you she didn't mean anything to me."

From the troubled expression on his face, I wasn't so sure about that. "But you meant something to her until her ambitions took a different turn."

Daniel was silent for a long moment. "What am I going to do for a crime reporter?"

"Hire someone new. There must be lots of people who studied journalism out there looking for work."

"Not for what I can pay them. That's how I ended up with Bianca. Only a student would take the job." He gave me a sideways look. "What about you?"

"I have a job."

"Yeah, but you're always saying how it's a job that leaves you with a lot of free time. Being a crime reporter just means going to the police station once a day at the most. If anything looks interesting the public relations officer will tell you. At the most, you interview the officer involved. You already have an in at the station."

"More of an out. The last thing the chief wants is to have me hanging around the station."

"He can't do much about it if you're a fully credentialed reporter."

My initial reaction was to say, *No, forget it. A bad idea.* But Chief Randal's threatening conversation of yesterday still rankled. This would be a means for me to have access to the department in such a way that he couldn't do much about it. And, although I didn't like to admit it, I did have a fair amount of free time. Real estate seemed to go in waves. One month I'd be very busy, then the next month I'd be the loneliest person in the world. I'd have to check with Maggie Fuller to see whether she was willing to share me with *The Sentinel*, but if she was willing, that might be one way for me to satisfy my continuing interest in law enforcement. But I wasn't going to give Daniel immediate satisfaction.

"I'll think about it," I said.

"That's all I ask. But let me know as soon as you decide because until I get someone I'll have to cover it myself."

"We'll have to negotiate my salary."

Daniel's face took on a troubled look.

"Only kidding," I said and laughed when he appeared deeply relieved.

Chapter Twenty-One

I was back at my desk brooding over how I was going to tell Maggie Fuller about my plan to take a part-time job. She had gone out of her way to hire me and get me trained for my realtor's license, so I felt an obligation toward her and didn't want to let her down. Plus I didn't want to completely give up real estate, I just felt a need to do something that would use my police training. All of this was preying on my mind when my cell phone rang. It was Dennis Harrington.

"I have a little more information on Owen Dragmore."

"Have you brought him in yet?"

"Nope. He didn't show up for work today, and he isn't at home. We're on the lookout for him."

"His wife said that he lived near one of his favorite watering holes, so if you check around the bars in his neighborhood, you might find him."

"We'll do that. We've also found out that he doesn't have a Firearms Identification Card, so if we find a rifle in his possession, we can bring him in and charge him."

"Let me know when you pick him up, and I'll come in and ID him as the guy who shot at me."

"Will do."

"I was wondering if there was any way I could get into Joseph Teller's office."

"I suppose so. What are you looking for?"

"Well, the chair of the English Department mentioned that Teller was investigating a possible case of student plagiarism. I forgot to tell you about it the last time we met because I was so focused on Dean Messing and Rockwell Boyd."

"Who was the student?" Detective Harrington asked, interested.

"No idea. Teller never told anyone. But I thought that if we searched his office we might be able to find the plagiarized paper."

"Finding a student paper in a teacher's office sounds like a needle in a haystack sort of thing. But, tell you what, I'm going to be in the neighborhood of the campus on something else in about an hour. Why don't we meet at the English Department, and I'll let you into Teller's office. We'll see what we can find."

"Sounds fine."

As soon as I ended the call, my desk phone rang. It was Roger Hastings.

"Marcie and I were checking on the Internet last night, and we've found a house in town that we'd like to take a look at."

I paused for a moment at the thought of the two of them being able to sit next to each other at a computer screen for more than five seconds. Perhaps fighting all the time didn't prevent them from scanning the web. I took down the information and promised to set something up for as soon as possible. I was about to check out the house myself on the computer when Maggie walked in the door. She waved a casual hello.

"Can I talk with you for a few moments?" I asked.

"Come," she said, turning and heading toward her

office.

I dutifully followed along and closed the door behind me. She settled in behind her desk and motioned for me to take a seat. She looked at me expectantly.

I decided the best approach was to charge right into it. "I've been thinking of working part-time as the crime reporter for *The Sentinel*. It wouldn't take up very much of my time most weeks, and I thought I could fit it around my responsibilities here."

I took a deep breath and realized my heart was beating rapidly. This was proving harder than I had thought. I felt such a sense of responsibility to Maggie for giving me a job that this felt like a betrayal.

"Dan Rencardi, who runs *The Sentinel*, is your boyfriend, isn't he?"

I didn't know how to answer. I wasn't sure that was true anymore.

"We go out together sometimes," I said.

Maggie raised an eyebrow as if somewhat surprised at the evasiveness of my reply.

"But that's not the reason I'm doing it," I said. "I've recently been working on a story about the death of a professor up at Minton State, and I find...well... I find that I've missed police work."

Maggie gave me a brief nod. "I wondered how long it would be before you found that being a realtor wasn't enough."

"It's not that it isn't enough—"

"Of course it is, and I don't blame you. When I left broadcasting for real estate, I spent the first few years bored out of my mind. Being a realtor is like being a bridesmaid or a midwife, someone else is always having all the thrills. I took any small job in media I

140

could find just to keep my hand in. It really wasn't until I opened my own agency that I found this work engaging enough for me to leave television completely." She smiled. "And even now, I'll admit, I get a little twinge once in a while. There's something very intoxicating about being in the public eye."

"It's not publicity that I'm looking for," I said, more than aware that this had been the chief's complaint against me.

"You're seeking excitement, and that's very much the same thing. Just like fame, it's addictive, and a desire for it can be very hard to break."

"Are you saying that's what I should do? Break my addiction? Forget about this idea of writing crime stories?"

She waved a languid hand. "No, I think right now this is exactly what you need, something to ease the transition to a civilian way of life. The real estate business isn't exactly booming these days. Once that picks up, and things get busier, you may find that it's easier to leave your old life behind." She paused as if unsure whether to continue. "From the very beginning, I've seen you as someone who would one day have her own agency, perhaps even take over this one. After all, I don't plan to do this forever. But you have a lot to learn yet, so you need to stay active in the business. This writing job will allow you to do that while satisfying your need for adventure. I'm sure we can work something out."

I got to my feet, still stunned by her suggestion that I might someday take over the agency. I'd thought of real estate primarily as a job, but suddenly I was beginning to think of it as a career.

"Thank you for being so understanding. Once I've arranged the details at *The Sentinel*, I'll let you know my schedule."

Maggie nodded and turned her attention to her computer.

I walked back to my desk and sat there, staring unseeing out at the green. Since leaving the police I had been pretty much reacting to events. I'd gone into real estate because Maggie had approached me with a job offer. I'd been going out with Daniel for six months because we'd started to date, and I liked him well enough. I'd suppressed my interest in police business because I didn't see any way to exercise it. Now I was suddenly confronted with options and a future that I could shape in just about any way I desired.

It was exciting but also overwhelming.

Chapter Twenty-Two

Dennis Harrington was already waiting for me when I arrived at the English Department office.

"Sorry to be late," I said.

"You're not. I got done with my business a little early and decided to do my waiting here."

Janet Phillips, who was alone in the office, glanced up as if she wasn't happy at having an officer of the law as a fixture, even for a brief period of time. I gave her a smile, and reluctantly, she nodded back.

Harrington held up a key. "Shall we?"

I followed him down the hall, around the corner, and down another hall to Professor Teller's door. The key worked smoothly, but the door still opened with a telltale squeak.

"They need to oil that hinge," Harrington said, handing me a pair of plastic gloves. "Where do you want to start?"

"Why don't you check the file cabinet, while I go through the desk?"

He nodded and went over to the gray metal set of file drawers that filled the corner of the room. I opened the middle drawer of the desk, which held primarily office supplies. The others I went through held grade books, old school announcements, and several file folders of notes. It wasn't until I reached the bottom drawer on the right-hand side that I found a manila folder with a two-page paper in it. At a brief glance, it looked to be a story about a young man living on his own, written in the form of a newspaper article. Behind the paper were the assignment directions and the date due. Apparently, it was to be handed in two weeks ago and was supposed to be a piece of student reporting for Teller's journalism class. Students were to interview someone about his or her life and write it up as a human interest article, changing the names to preserve anonymity. As I read more closely, I learned that this story was about a college student from a chaotic home living on his own by working multiple jobs and barely scraping together enough money to pay tuition. It was a powerful, gripping piece, and the byline was one I knew: Evan Miller. Evan Miller, the blond-haired guy who planned to become a college professor because journalism was too gritty for him.

I called Harrington over and showed it to him.

"Do you think that's the plagiarized paper?" he said dubiously. "Maybe Teller just kept it because it was a great piece of work."

I shook my head. "It's not even graded. I think Teller hung on to it because he was going to check and see if it was cribbed from the Internet. I know this student, and he plans to go on to graduate school. If a charge of plagiarism were proven against him it could devastate his chances for continuing with his education. He'd have trouble getting good recommendations when it got around the faculty, and if he were expelled from the course, it would show on his transcript."

"Okay, so you think this Evan guy came to Teller and wanted to be let off the hook. Teller refused, so the kid pushed him out the window."

"Evan is certainly big enough. I could see them getting into a fight that might end up that way. I'm not saying the student came here intending for that to happen, but from what I've heard, Teller could be irascible. If the kid was desperate, maybe one thing led to another."

"Then why didn't the kid take the paper?"

"It was in a bottom drawer, not that easy to find. Or maybe he panicked when Teller went out the window and ran away without looking."

Harrington took the paper and the assignment directions and placed them in a large plastic evidence envelope he pulled from his pocket.

"You said this guy is an English major. Do you think they'd have his address in the Department Office?"

"Definitely worth a shot."

We retraced our steps back to the English Department and walked up to Janet Phillips' desk. Fiona Halsey was in the office now, too, her long hair curtaining her face as she sat at her desk reading through some mail. She didn't glance up at us.

"Would you be able to tell me where Evan Miller lives?" Harrington asked.

"Evan? What's he done?" Phillips asked, looking concerned.

"We'd just like the opportunity to talk to him," the detective said with an encouraging smile.

"I'm not really supposed to give out that sort of information without the student's permission."

"Perhaps you could make an exception for a murder investigation?"

The woman thought for a brief moment then

pressed some keys on her computer.

"He's in Farrow Hall, Room 213."

"Where would that be?"

Phillips gave us directions, looking unhappy the entire time. "I'm sure you're mistaken about Evan having anything to do with this," she said. "He's a senior English major and probably the best student we've seen in many years. He has a good chance of getting into one of the Ivies for graduate school."

Harrington gave her a reassuring smile. "We just need some information from him. There's nothing to be concerned about."

Phillips looked unconvinced. I figured she'd seen lots of police shows and could probably hear beyond the rhetoric.

"Who is Evan's faculty advisor?" I asked her.

She glanced at the screen again. "Professor Boyd."

I nodded and resisted catching Harrington's eye.

"Are you going to go over to talk with Evan?" I asked as we walked down the stairs to the front door of Dillard Hall.

He nodded. "Want to come along?"

"Sure," I said, surprised at the invitation.

"You know him already. A familiar face might convince him to cooperate. But you have to promise not to write about any of this without my permission."

"Agreed. But we can't very well accuse him of plagiarism without evidence."

"I don't plan to accuse him of anything. I'm just going to ask him where he was at the time of Teller's death, and I'm going to try to find out why the professor had his paper in the drawer of his desk."

We followed the secretary's directions and found

ourselves in front of a contemporary looking building. We walked in the front door. A guy sitting at a desk glanced up.

"Can I help you?" he asked, sounding more friendly than hostile.

"We're here to talk to one of your residents," Detective Harrington said, showing his badge.

"Sure…I guess so. I'm supposed to keep strangers out, but I guess that doesn't apply to the police."

Harrington grinned. "No, I guess not."

"Do you know where you're going?"

"We'll find our way."

We walked down the hall to the stairwell and went up to the second floor. We stopped in front of 213 and Harrington knocked.

"Who is it," a muffled voice asked.

"The police."

The springs of a bed squeaked and a few seconds later the door opened and a short, curly-headed boy wearing glasses peered out at us.

"Did you say 'the police'?"

"That's right," Harrington said. "May we come in?

The kid slowly backed out of the doorway, and we entered. It was a small room and somewhat schizophrenic. On one side was an unmade bed with several books piled on top. Various items of clothing were strewn on the floor, and there was a general sense of clutter. On a bedside table was a chocolate cake with a plastic fork stuck in it.

The other side of the room had a bed with a colorful coverlet that was tucked in with military precision. Only one book lay on an end table by the bed, and there wasn't a sign of dirty clothes. I wondered how well this odd couple got along.

"You are?"

"Seth. Seth Kronin," he said, going over to stand by the messy bed as if to show what side of the room was his. I wouldn't have been so proud.

"Evan Miller is your roommate?"

An obvious expression of relief passed over Seth's face as he realized the bell hadn't tolled for him.

"That's right."

"Have you been roommates long?"

He shook his head. "Only since the start of the semester."

"Were you friends before that?"

"No. I didn't know him."

"Isn't that a little unusual?" I said. "By senior year don't most students have good friends they want to room with?"

The boy shrugged. "I suppose. I've sort of floated around for four years—a different roommate every year, sometimes every semester."

From his domestic habits, I could see why.

"And Evan was supposed to have a room to himself because he's an honor student, but at the last minute, the University had a shortage of rooms, so I got put in with him. I don't think he was very happy about it."

"Do you know where Evan would be right now?" Harrington asked.

"I think he's got a class. I didn't hear him leave. I was still sleeping."

Harrington nodded and handed Seth a card. "Would you have Evan give me a call when he gets in? And could you give me your cell phone number?"

"Why?" the boy asked, looking worried again.

"Just so I can give you a call to see if Evan came back."

"Okay…sure." Seth recited a number, and Harrington put it into his phone.

"Is Evan in trouble about something?" Seth asked. He seemed pleased at the thought. I figured living with Mr. Perfect could get tiresome.

Harrington shook his head. "We just want to ask him a few questions about an incident on campus."

"But you're the real police, not campus security?"

"That's right."

I could see his mind calculating that this had to be something serious. I was sure he wanted to ask more. Before he could, Harrington turned, and we left the room.

"Imagine living with that guy for twelve weeks," Harrington said, walking down the hall. "I'd be checking myself for fleas."

"Do you want to see if Janet Phillips can tell us where Evan Miller's class is? We could go talk to him when he gets out."

"It's tempting, but I think I'd rather have him come down to the station than question him in a public hallway."

"You don't think he'll run?"

"Where would he go? Plus he's got a future. If he's as smart as I think he is, he'll try to bluff his way out of this, if he is guilty."

I didn't agree, but he was the boss.

"Do you think we should try to find out if that story really is plagiarized?"

"How would we go about doing that?" he asked.

"Rockwell Boyd is Miller's adviser. Why not bring the paper to him? He might know how to use the Internet to check on something like that."

"Good idea. Let me take the paper back to the station and place it into evidence. Then I'll make a copy of it. Maybe you should be the one to bring it to Boyd. It might seem less threatening that way."

Although I wasn't really anxious to talk with Boyd again after our last conversation, I wanted to see his face when I mentioned his encounter with Teller in the restaurant.

"Would it be okay to tell Boyd that I know Teller spotted him cheating on the dean?"

"Sure. It might rattle him into saying something we can use. We have to follow up on that angle as well. We don't know for sure that this plagiarism issue had anything to do with Teller's death."

We walked back to our cars, enjoying the stroll across the campus.

"Kids don't realize how lucky they have it," Harrington said, watching the crowds pass by.

"In some ways. But I think being young is overrated. You have a lot of worries: passing courses, getting a job, and finding a stable relationship."

"Sure, but when you're young life is still filled with possibilities. You've got options."

I glanced over at the detective, surprised by his philosophical tone. "Do you have regrets about your choices?"

"Not when it comes to relationships. But when it comes to a job…" He shrugged.

"You wanted to do something else."

"Actually I wanted to be a veterinarian. I always

loved animals."

"What happened?"

"I had an older brother who wanted to be a doctor, and my parents sent him on to a really good college."

"So there was no money left for you?" I asked, thinking about how this was just the reverse of my family.

"I could have gone on to a state school, I guess. I'd have been able to pay most of my own way. But when you've got a really talented older brother, you don't want to compete with him on the same playing field."

"You mean school?"

"Right. He was a really bookish kind of guy, while I was into sports and doing stuff. I knew I could be a better cop than he ever would. So I avoided the competition."

"And now you regret it."

"Not every day or even most of the time. But once in a while I wonder how I would have turned out if I'd become a vet. I think I might be a nicer person."

"The world needs cops, too."

He smiled. "And real estate agents turned reporters."

"I suppose."

He reached his car and stood by the door. "I'll give you a call when we pick up Dragmore. I have a feeling that even if he had nothing to do with Teller's death he's been up to something we can grab him for doing."

I thanked Harrington and opened my car door, wondering if I was going to become a nicer person because I was no longer a cop.

Chapter Twenty-Three

When I got back to the office, I dropped off my things and walked up the street where I got a salad to go from Angie's, a breakfast and lunch place nearby. I ate at my desk while I tried to get in touch with the realtor handling the house the Hastings had found on the Internet. I finally got through to her, and she told me the combination to the lockbox on the door. She sounded very pleased that I had interested clients and broadly hinted that the sellers were motivated and open to negotiating the price. I called Roger at his work number, and he curtly informed me that they'd meet me at my office at seven o'clock. No cordial thanks given for my time or effort. I came away hoping that this would be the house that rid me of the Hastings once and for all.

I had just finished my salad when Daniel called.

"I was wondering if you could stop in at *The Sentinel* later on this afternoon, and we could put the finishing touches on the story about Teller."

"I thought we were going to string that out to give us an excuse to keep investigating his death."

"Well, Bianca turned in a pretty comprehensive first draft, if we restrict ourselves to covering the high points of his life. And really, how good are the chances that we're going to find out what actually happened in his office that afternoon?"

"Pretty good, I'd say." His sudden lack of confidence stung.

"Even without Bianca's source."

Bianca again.

I gave him a quick overview of what I had discovered about Marge Rowen's husband, Teller's meeting with Boyd in the Northampton restaurant, and Evan Miller's possible plagiarism.

"You have made progress," he said, the surprise evident in his voice.

"I *was* a cop," I said with asperity.

"Sorry, I didn't mean to offend you."

I took a deep breath. "No problem."

"But I think we should get this biographical story about Teller out there this week. It will keep readers interested, so they won't forget his death. If we do find out how he died, we can always follow up with another piece. How does that sound?"

"Fine. I can be done here in half an hour. How about if I come over then, so we'll have the afternoon to work on it?"

Daniel agreed, and after making a few more calls on real estate listings, I said goodbye to Molly, who was covering the phones, and made my way to *The Sentinel* offices. When I walked into the lobby, Myra smiled and gave me thumbs up.

"So you got rid of her," she whispered. "Good work."

"Actually, I got a lot of help from her parents after she got hit on the head. They didn't want her to have any more to do with journalism."

"And she listened to her parents?"

"Sort of. I think now she's got her mind set on

going into television."

Myra rolled her eyes. "I wouldn't trust that one any further than I could throw her."

I heard Daniel come down the hall from his office. He had a big smile on his face and gave me a hug.

"Good to see you," he said. "Let's see what we can do to preserve Joe Teller's legacy."

I nodded, and he led me into the conference room. I sat down on Daniel's immediate right, taking the spot that Bianca had usually occupied.

Daniel turned to me with anticipation. "What have you decided about taking over as police reporter?"

"I discussed it with Maggie Fuller, and she's willing to give me the time if I really want to do it."

"And do you?"

"I've given it some thought. I think it's something I'd like to do right now. I can't promise you how long I'll want to stay with it. But I kind of miss police work, and this would be one way to stay partially connected. If you still want me, that is?"

Daniel reached over and squeezed my arm. "Of course, I do."

I had a bad feeling that he meant this in a more personal way. I debated telling him that I'd been rethinking our relationship but decided that would make it very awkward for us to work together on the Teller article. Better to put that discussion off to a future date. He took a copy of Bianca's story out of a manila folder. I could see that he had already written in additions and emendations. He read the story out loud to me paragraph by paragraph, and we discussed each one line by line. It was all very comfortable and companionable. I had to admit that Bianca had done a good job researching Teller's background in journalism and his accomplishments at Minton State. Between the foundation she had laid and Daniel's changes, it was a fine piece. All I asked was that it be made clear that Teller's death was still under investigation by the police. I knew Detective Harrington would have no objection to our saying that, and it would leave the door open to a future story that I hoped to write solving the crime.

"You have no objection to this story coming out under your joint byline with Bianca's name first?"

"Actually, I have no problem with it coming out over her name alone. After all, she's the one who actually wrote it. It will be kind of her swan song." I figured I could afford to be magnanimous now that I'd won.

"That's very generous of you. I'm sure Bianca will appreciate it."

I doubted that, but it seemed the right thing to do.

My cell phone rang. I saw that it was Detective Harrington calling me. I apologized to Daniel and took the call.

"We picked up Dragmore at a bar in his neighborhood just like you predicted. We got lucky. He was half in the bag and started ranting about how much he hated Teller, and how *The Sentinel* was going to make some kind of hero out of him. He even mentioned your name. Not only that, but he had the rifle prominently displayed on the gun rack in his truck. With no FIC we can take the rifle away and hit him with a fine. If you come down and identify him, we'll see what we can do about upping the charges."

I told him I'd come down to the station right away.

When I hung up, Daniel gave me a long look.

"What was that all about?"

I gave him a brief summary of Dragmore's relationship with Teller and his taking a pot shot at me.

Daniel furrowed his brow. "He shot at you, and you didn't tell me?"

"I didn't want to worry you. You had a lot on your mind with Teller dying and the attack on Bianca."

"But still. This is something I should have known."

I shrugged. "I was lucky. No harm, no foul," I said, with more casualness than I felt.

Daniel stared at me as if he hardly knew me. "You could have been killed."

"I wasn't, and that's the important thing."

"I can't believe you're so unconcerned about this."

I stood up and paused. I gave him a level look. "I'm not unconcerned. In fact, I'm going over to the police station right now, and I'm hoping to get the book thrown at this guy. But I'm not going to panic about it and run crying to my boyfriend. I'm more professional than that."

"I'm not asking you to be unprofessional, but you could have told me when it happened. I hope the next time you will."

"Since I've never been shot at before, I doubt there will be a repeat."

"You were almost shot at once before."

"But I wasn't, and now that I'm no longer a cop the chances are minimal."

I walked out the door before Daniel could stand up to show me out. Myra gave me a quizzical glance as I strode through the lobby, but I didn't meet her eye. I knew I was being unreasonable, but that was the way I felt. Daniel couldn't get all misty eyed about Bianca, and at the same time expect me to rely on him for support.

I kept walking purposefully right up to Main Street and into the police station. The desk sergeant glanced up and recognized me. He picked up the phone, and a couple of minutes later, Detective Harrington came out into the lobby and brought me in.

"So far he claims to know nothing about Teller's death," the detective said as we walked down the hall. "He says he was at work that afternoon. We called over to the auto body shop where he works, and the manager confirmed it. But I sent over a couple of officers to talk to the people at the shop to see if anyone can state that they saw him there that afternoon."

"Probably hard for people to remember the exact day. All the afternoons probably tend to blend together."

Harrington nodded. "I've set up an impromptu lineup in the first interview room. You can see them through the one-way mirror. Just tell me if you see the guy who took a shot at you."

I nodded. I felt a nervous tightening in my belly. I'd guided witnesses through lineups before. I'd even been in one once with a woman accused of shoplifting. But there was something about being put on the spot to identify someone and possibly send him to jail that made me tense up. I told myself that I'd had a good look at the shooter, and I would know his weasel-like face anywhere.

Harrington and I walked into the interview room. Jim Russell, Harrington's partner, was already there, and he gave me a nod. I faced a yellow curtain that

157

covered the mirror. Russell went over and pulled a string and the curtain drew back revealing a room with five men standing in line staring at me. Although I knew they couldn't see me, I still felt that each one was looking me right in the eye. I carefully studied each face, moving from left to right. They had done a good job of getting men of similar characteristics. All were thin, and although there were differences in height, the range was narrow, and each man looked fully capable of trying to shoot someone in the back. Despite the similarities, it only took me one time down the line to spot the man who had taken a shot at me.

"It's number four," I said.

"Are you sure?" Harrington asked.

"Absolutely."

Harrington turned to his partner. "Jim, take Kate back to the lobby."

I started to walk to the door.

"Kate, if you could wait in the lobby for a few minutes, I'd like to talk to you after we have a chat with Mr. Dragmore."

"Is that who I picked out?" I asked.

Harrington grinned. "Right on target."

Feeling like a satisfied citizen, I followed Jim back to the lobby. I sat there for a while checking my e-mail and returning a couple of phone calls. I was just starting to get bored and wonder why the police didn't put any magazines out as a public service when Harrington came back and motioned for me to follow him. We went down the hall and into his cubicle. Harrington settled down behind his desk.

"I'd like to see him charged with attempted murder, but the DA would probably never go along. It would be too hard to prove that he intended to kill you. He's already claiming that he was just shooting at a squirrel in the corn field and the shot went high."

"If we brought up his argument with Teller, it would speak to his motive in wanting to keep me from writing a story about the man."

Harrington shrugged. "Probably too complicated to prove. Anyway, firing a gun near a residence is enough to get him in a lot of trouble. There will be a hefty fine and jail time. Of course, he'll probably get probation, but with his tendency to get into trouble he'll probably violate his probation and end up in jail within a matter of months. Don't worry, he'll pay for what he did."

"What did the officers find out at his place of employment?"

"Unfortunately, a couple of his co-workers remember that he was definitely there that day. They could be lying, of course, but the cops who talked to them didn't think Dragmore was popular enough that anyone would lie for him. He's not exactly the kind of guy who makes friends wherever he goes."

I paused and thought it all over. "You know, I could never really see Dragmore killing Teller on campus. He isn't the kind of guy who thinks things through. He might wait outside his wife's house some night if Teller was there and try to jump him, but he wouldn't be able to formulate a coherent plan."

"He probably isn't sober enough most of the time to work one out."

"That leaves us with two suspects whose whereabouts at the time of the murder are unaccounted for: Rockwell Boyd and Evan Miller," I said.

"I called our little friend Seth Kronin again, and

apparently Evan Miller never came back to his room after class. That might not mean anything. He could be working in the library or hanging out with some friends, I suppose."

"Or he could be in the wind," I suggested.

"Yeah, maybe he somehow got word we were looking for him. I wouldn't trust this Kronin kid not to tip him off."

"They didn't seem to be friends."

Harrington shrugged. "Well, I doubt he's gone far. He has to show up for class if he still wants to get into graduate school. We'll find him eventually. I should have listened to you and grabbed him in the hall."

Harrington handed me a manila folder.

"Why don't you go have that chat with Rockwell Boyd? See what he says about his advisee's plagiarism and about his own extracurricular cheating on the dean."

"I'll get right on it tomorrow. By the way, I'm going to be taking over the crime beat for *The Sentinel*."

"Bianca's had enough?"

"Her parents have. So I'll be coming in every day to check for anything newsworthy."

"Does the chief know?"

"Doesn't he know everything?"

"He won't be happy."

"He's not happy that I still live in town. I guess he'll just have to learn to live with it."

Harrington smiled. He stood up and reached a hand across his desk.

"Thanks for coming in. I appreciate it. And let me say that I'm happy that Dragmore wasn't more sober or a better shot the other afternoon."

"So am I," I said, feeling my stomach clenching again.

Chapter Twenty-Four

The Hastings sat in my car without speaking for the ten-minute trip to the house they wanted to see. I was obviously the recipient of the silent aftermath of an argument they'd had on the way over. Neither one could bear to look at the other, so I was reconciled to the idea that this was going to be another unsuccessful showing. My hopes sank even more when we pulled up in front of the house, and I saw that it was a mid-century modern: a nineteen-fifties ranch that might have made my grandparents nostalgic but would do nothing for the Hastings. And, indeed, as we went up the walk, they were grim-faced as if facing joint root canal.

I fumbled around with the lock box and finally managed to extract the key. I opened the door, and we entered into a small, low-ceilinged entryway that seemed to have been designed for munchkins. I was expecting them to suggest that we immediately turn around and leave, but perhaps their earlier argument had taken all the fight out of them because they remained silent. We walked down the hall. Suddenly the space expanded and we were in a room that ran half the length of the house with a ceiling that soared up to the roof. A large stone fireplace dominated the far wall, giving the room a definite Frank Lloyd Wright flair. We were all silent, a bit stunned by the contrast between the claustrophobic entry and this grand room.

"It's amazing," Marcie whispered in a worshipful voice.

I didn't respond, waiting for Roger's sarcastic comeback.

"It certainly is," he said fervently.

I turned to look at him to see if he was sincere, but the expression of rapture on his face left no doubt. They had fallen in love with the house. Sometimes that's the way it happens. Usually, one person or the other is enchanted and the other is indifferent, but there are those rare times when a house is mutually captivating. I hoped the emotion they were feeling in this room would be enough to compensate for what—from my limited experience with homes of this period—was bound to be a small dated kitchen and tiny bedrooms.

That was the way it seemed to work. The Hastings dismissed the major limitations of the kitchen with a few casual comments about how the price of the home would enable them to extensively redo it. Similarly, they seemed happy to envision modernizing the pokey bathrooms, and they didn't blink an eye at the barely functional bedrooms. At the end of our tour, they turned to me in unison and almost stumbled over each other in announcing that they wanted to make an offer. I pointed out that the price of the house was most likely negotiable, and right on the spot, while still gazing at the cathedral ceiling, we came to an acceptable offering at almost full price. In fact, the Hastings actually looked at each other and smiled. For the first time, I could imagine how they had looked on their wedding day.

"We hope they accept our offer," Marcie said. "I love this house."

"I'll do my best," I said. I'd learned never to promise more than I'm sure to deliver in this business.

Roger actually put an arm around Marcie's waist and smiled. "If they want more, we'll find a way to come up with it," he said, giving her hip a bump.

She looked at him gratefully. I was starting to feel like I was intruding on an intimate moment. They insisted on signing the offering forms even though I hadn't filled them out yet because they wanted me to fax them out immediately the next morning. I had to almost drag them out of the house and back to the car because they were already gushing about where their furniture would go in the great room. When we got to my office, they left me a check and made me promise again that I would submit their offer first thing in the morning in case there were competitive bids. As I watched them drive away, for once not shouting at each other, I hoped that they would still feel the same when they woke up tomorrow.

It seemed that the battle of Hastings had come to a conclusion.

Chapter Twenty-Five

During my run the next morning I reflected happily on last night. Though I didn't want to prematurely count my chickens, I had a good feeling that this sale was going to work out. So as not to tempt fate, I rushed through my shower and breakfast in order to get down to the office and put in their offer. By nine o'clock all the paperwork had been done and sent out. I sat back in my chair, feeling like I'd already done a day's work when Nancy Bryant walked in for her scheduled phone duty.

"What are you doing here so early?" she asked in amazement.

"I wanted to submit the Hastings offer."

Nancy gaped. "They actually made an offer on something? Did you have to buy it for them?"

"Actually, they fell in love with a mid-century modern up by the park. Can you believe it?"

"Mid-century," she screwed up her face. "It probably has electric heat and windows that leak cold air like a sieve."

"Right you are, but nothing is going to turn the course of true love."

"Speaking of true love, I heard that you're going to be taking on the job of crime reporter."

"Where did you hear that?"

"It's around town."

I wondered if Maggie had spread the word. It would be like her to think that having me working on *The Sentinel* would make me more popular and help bring in clients.

"The story is true, but I didn't do it for love."

"Why, then?"

"I missed working with the police, and I thought this would be a way of getting involved."

"Is this going to get you in trouble with Maggie?"

"She's all right with it."

Nancy raised an eyebrow in surprise. "You said love had nothing to do with it, but I'm sure the chance to work with Daniel must have influenced you a little bit."

I paused, not sure how much I wanted to share with Nancy. Finally deciding that I needed someone to talk to, I continued, "I think Daniel and I are about at the end of the line, so Daniel's being involved is actually a reason not to do it."

"If you break up that could be awkward."

"I guess I'm hoping that we're both mature enough to have a successful working relationship even if our personal one has ended."

Nancy gave me a dubious look, then her phone rang, and she scurried over to her desk to answer it. I decided that it was time for me to call the English Department and find out when I could meet with Rockwell Boyd. I called and got Janet Phillips, who told me that Boyd was scheduled for an office hour at the end of his next class.

"I received a call from Detective Harrington this morning," she said. "Apparently, Evan Miller hasn't been staying in his dorm room lately. The detective asked if I knew where he might be. I had to tell him they were dorm rooms, not prison cells. Students can come and go as they please. We don't keep track of them."

"But surely if someone disappeared, you would try to find out where he was."

"Of course, but he could just be staying somewhere else for a day or two. Detective Harrington asked me for the contact information on his parents. We really aren't supposed to give that out without the student's permission, but I thought that under the circumstances…"

"Since it was related to a murder investigation?"

"Yes. He also wanted to know the names of any of Evan's friends, but I just don't know that sort of thing. I told him to get back in touch with Evan's roommate."

I figured that would be a dead end.

"Well, I'm sure you did the right thing."

"I ran it by Professor Franks, and she thought I did just right."

I told her that I would be there in half an hour to catch Professor Boyd in his office. She warned me not to get my hopes up because, as she had told me before, he didn't always keep his assigned office hours. After I hung up the phone, I sat there for a moment considering the likelihood that Evan Miller had killed Teller. In my brief acquaintance with him, he had seemed like a nice kid, normal and well balanced if a bit shy. Of course, if he and Teller got into an argument, it was possible that passions had been raised on both sides that had led to violence. Miller could have gotten desperate as he saw his future slipping away. But since no one had seen him in the hall that day, even if he had motive it was going to be hard to prove that he had the opportunity. Of course, there was always a chance that since he wasn't a hardened criminal, under questioning he might break down and confess.

I got to my feet and headed for the door.

"I'm going to be out for a little while," I said to Nancy.

"Got a showing?"

"No, I've got to question an annoying little professor about a case of plagiarism."

She rolled her eyes. "You do get the best jobs."

Chapter Twenty-Six

This time when Rockwell Boyd came down the hall and saw me standing in front of his office door, he wasn't nearly so flirty. An expression of dismay mixed with annoyance passed over his face. He looked me over as if something unsavory had turned up unexpectedly on his doorstep.

"What are you here about this time, Ms. Cameron?" he asked, unlocking his office door. He marched inside and sat behind his desk. He didn't indicate that I could sit down, but I did so anyway.

"Are you aware that Joseph Teller was investigating one of your advisees for plagiarism?"

He smiled scornfully. "I have twenty advisees. It's the curse of being a popular teacher that students request me. Given Teller's obsession with plagiarism, I'm not surprised that one of my advisees would be in his sights."

"Would you be surprised to know that it was Evan Miller?"

His head jerked back as if someone had slapped him. "Evan? I don't believe it. Not only does he take scholarship too seriously, but he wouldn't risk his future as an academic by plagiarizing."

"Why was Evan taking an Introduction to Journalism course in the first place?" I asked.

"Because it's a requirement for the English major.

A silly one in my opinion, but Teller got it put through the faculty senate many years ago, and once approved, requirements are almost impossible to change. Now that Teller is gone maybe we can get it dropped."

"So Evan might feel that Journalism was an unimportant course that he had to do well in only because it was part of his major. Since I know for a fact that journalism isn't an interest of his, he might well have decided to take a shortcut and steal a paper. Even the best student may sometimes cut corners."

Boyd shook his head vehemently. "There has to be another explanation."

I took a copy of Evan's paper out of my jacket pocket and handed it across the desk. Reluctantly he took it. "The police and I found this in Professor Teller's desk. It's supposed to be a student newspaper story based on a personal interview. I believe Teller thought it was either made up or plagiarized from the Internet."

Boyd glanced at the paper. "How do you know this was the paper?"

"I know from Professor Franks that he was considering bringing plagiarism charges against one of his students. This paper, which probably should have been returned to Evan over a week ago, was found in his desk. That leads me to believe that Teller held on to it for further consideration."

"Isn't that what the police would call circumstantial evidence?"

"Which is often the best kind."

"What does Miller himself say about all this?"

"He's disappeared. The police are looking for him as we speak."

Boyd looked across the room then down at the pages in his hand. "If Evan made this up out of whole cloth—if it's truly a work of fiction—we'll never be able to prove it."

"Probably not. But if he stole if off of the Internet wouldn't you be able to find out?"

"There are computer programs that enable a teacher to check on things like that. The Department subscribes to one and makes it available to the faculty."

"Would you be willing to do that?"

He paused.

"Don't you want to know if Evan Miller is a plagiarist? After all, I'm sure he expects you to write him a letter of recommendation. Wouldn't this be highly relevant to your evaluation?"

Boyd gave me a penetrating look. "It's not quite as simple as that, is it?"

"What do you mean?"

"If I give you evidence that Miller plagiarized this paper, I also give you a reason to arrest him for murder. Then I'm caught in the middle between the police and a student. I can imagine myself being sued by the boy's parents for violating confidentiality if he gets arrested for murder."

I shrugged. "Suit yourself. The police can find an expert to do the checking for them. I just thought you might want to see if this case can be settled quickly before we have to probe other possibilities further. Ones that might be more awkward for you personally."

"What are you talking about?" he asked, irritated.

"We know that Joseph Teller saw you with a boyfriend up at a restaurant in Northampton. The police are considering whether you might have been afraid that Teller would mention this to the dean as a way of keeping his job. Knowing you were cheating on him might have made the dean less likely to work hard to keep you on the faculty. That would give you a pretty good motive for silencing Teller."

"Are you trying to coerce me into checking on Evan's paper by threatening to tell the dean about my luncheon?" he asked. He tried to smile confidently, but it was a struggle.

I spread my hands and put my most innocent expression on my face. "Of course not, that would be wrong. I'm just saying that the clock is ticking on this investigation, and if we can't follow up rapidly on Evan, we may have to pursue the hypothesis that you killed Teller, so he wouldn't spill the beans to your dean. That would involve having another conversation with Dean Messing."

"Don't be silly. That fellow I had lunch with was just an old friend, I can easily explain it to the dean."

"Have you told him about that luncheon?" I asked.

Boyd shifted nervously in his chair. "Not yet."

"Too bad. It would have sounded more convincing if it had come sooner."

"But I had no reason to kill Teller. He wouldn't have told the dean about seeing me in that restaurant. That wasn't the kind of guy Teller was. He had a sort of old school integrity."

"An integrity you intended to abuse by taking his job," I snapped.

Boyd shrugged. "Jobs in the humanities are hard to come by. This might be my only opportunity to get tenure."

"I doubt you'll have much of a chance of getting

the job with the suspicion that you murdered Teller hanging over your head. And that's right where it will be unless we have proof that Evan Miller is the killer."

"So my only hope of not having further accusations come my way is to investigate this plagiarism matter."

I nodded. "It looks like it."

"I'll still have to think about this. It puts me in an awkward legal position."

I stood up and smiled. "Take all the time you want, just remember that Detective Harrington is getting impatient, and he may decide to talk to Dean Messing at any time."

I turned to walk away.

"I thought you were just a real estate agent turned amateur reporter, not an enforcer for the police," Boyd said in an aggrieved tone.

I glanced back at him. "I am a reporter, and I'm doing what reporters try to do: find out the truth about what happened."

He snorted. "You don't care about truth. You just want the most sensational story because it will sell newspapers."

"I think you have *The Sentinel* mixed up with some tabloid. We cover the local news for local people. If we don't get it right, everyone quickly comes to find out about it. So we have to stick to the truth."

I didn't know where all of that came from, but for the moment at least it sounded good and made me feel better as I went out the door.

I was strutting down the hall pretty proud of myself when my cell phone rang. It took me a moment before I recognized that the choked voice on the other end was Daniel's. At first, I couldn't understand what he was saying.

"Could you repeat that?" I asked.

"Bianca's dead," he said in something between an angry shout and a sob.

Chapter Twenty-Seven

I sat in a chair in front of Detective Harrington's desk. He was leafing through a manila folder. Daniel was slumped in a chair beside me. Manila folders were where evidence resided until put into the computer.

I looked over at Daniel, but he didn't meet my eye. We had arrived at the police station at the same time but hardly spoke during the five minutes we spent together in the lobby. Daniel was the picture of pain, and although he hadn't directly accused me, I felt that somehow I was partly to blame for Bianca's death. It was true I hadn't liked her much and suspected her of trying to steal my boyfriend, but looked at objectively, I'd been the one who tried to get her to stop meddling in a murder case. I had tried to protect her. Somehow, however, that didn't make me feel less guilty.

"How did she die?" Daniel asked.

"Like I told you on the phone, she was found dead in her dorm room at nine o'clock last night. Her roommate was away for the day and found her when she returned. The preliminary report we have on the cause of death is that she was smothered, possibly with her own pillow."

"Was anyone seen in the area of her dorm room that night?" I asked.

He shook his head. "But the time of death could be anywhere from four o'clock to seven. During that time many of the students would have been over in the dining hall for dinner."

"What about the door monitor? Did he see Bianca come in with anyone?"

"No. But apparently, there was a lapse in security after four. The scheduled monitor couldn't cover—he had to study for a big lab exam or something—and the person who was supposed to take over from him didn't get the message. She only showed up at seven. So we have a three-hour gap."

"Bianca lived on an all girl floor. Didn't anyone notice a man up there?" Daniel said angrily.

"Why do you assume it was a man?" I asked.

"She was suffocated. Bianca was a healthy young woman. It would have taken someone a lot stronger to suffocate her."

Harrington glanced at me and shrugged. We'd both seen a fair number of tough women in our time.

"No one noticed a man or a woman going into her dorm room," he answered.

"When was she released from the hospital?" I asked.

"Yesterday at around noon," Daniel said in a dull voice.

I stared at him.

"Bianca called me just before she left the hospital," he added, giving me a defensive look.

"What did she say?" Harrington asked.

He sighed. "She said that she had one more idea she wanted to follow up on regarding the Teller case."

"And you told her not to do it. That she should leave it to the police, didn't you?" I asked.

He stared at the floor. "I told her that she was no

longer the crime reporter for *The Sentinel*, that I had given the job to you. So she should tell me whatever she knew, and I would pass it on to you."

"What did she say?" I asked.

"She hung up on me." Daniel stared across the room. "That was the last time I spoke to her."

Neither Harrington nor I said anything. We both knew that what Daniel told her had been like throwing kerosene on the flames of her competitiveness. I was the person who had beaten her out for Daniel's attention and now for her job. All that was left to Bianca was to scoop me on the Teller story and prove she was a better reporter than I'd ever be. I was sure that had driven her to take dangerous chances. She had probably gone right back to her secret source who had proven to be more deeply involved in the murder than Bianca had suspected. Could it have been Rockwell Boyd? As an English major Bianca was sure to have had him in class. If he had thought she was going to pursue this to the bitter end, he might have killed her. Or possibly it could have been Evan Miller. Maybe she knew where he was hiding and talked to him.

"Did you find out anything about whom she might have talked to on campus yesterday?" I asked Harrington.

"We got a copy of her class schedule and talked to her professors. She had classes yesterday at one and two and went to both. We know because she spoke to both teachers after class to get any work she might have missed while in the hospital. When those classes meet again tomorrow, we'll send in an officer to ask the students if anyone had a conversation with her."

"What about Evan Miller? Do you have any word

on where he might be?"

Harrington shook his head. "We talked to his roommate again, but he hasn't seen him. He skipped his classes yesterday. We called his parents—they live right here in town—but they haven't seen him in several days. He never talked to them about having any problem with one of his professors."

"The parents are always the last to know," I said.

Daniel's eyes lit up with a desire for vengeance. "This Evan Miller sure sounds like a good suspect. Look at all he had to lose. Bianca would probably trust another student a lot more than faculty. She would probably never expect him to harm her." He turned to Harrington. "You have to find this guy."

"We're doing the best we can," Harrington said. "We asked his parents for the names of his friends. We checked with the students he sat next to and asked his teachers to contact us if he showed up for class. We called the president of the Poetry and Literature Club to see if she had any ideas. So far nothing has panned out."

Daniel shook his head. "He's got to be somewhere. Probably hiding with a girlfriend."

"If he has one, we haven't found out about her yet," said Harrington.

"Is there anything I can do?" Daniel asked, the frustration coming off him in waves.

"Why don't you go back to your office and just think about all the conversations you had with Bianca. Try to recall if there was anyone special she mentioned."

Daniel jumped to his feet. "Don't you think that's all I've been thinking about since you called? Now I have to go back to my office and write another story about a murder on campus."

"Just keep it vague," Harrington warned. "Say it was due to unknown causes and is under investigation."

"Don't worry, I know the drill. Cover up is the phrase of the day," Daniel snapped. He turned and without looking at me, marched out of the office.

Harrington raised a quizzical eyebrow.

"He's upset. They were rather close," I offered.

"Don't take this the wrong way, but do you think that she and Daniel might have had a lovers' falling out? A lot of times those situations lead to violence."

I took a deep breath. Although I hadn't put it into words even to myself, the thought had briefly crossed my mind. Even considering it made me feel disloyal to Daniel.

"I don't think it ever went that far. Daniel's really not the type."

Harrington shrugged as if to say all men were the type.

"Did Bianca's parents say anything about suing the newspaper or Daniel?" I asked.

"They were too upset to say much of anything. But, since *The Sentinel* technically no longer employed Bianca at her time of death, I'd say Daniel is probably off the hook. However, he would be wise to have the newspaper's lawyer look into it."

I changed the subject and filled him in on my conversation with Rockwell Boyd.

"Do you think he'll help us find out if the paper was plagiarized?" Harrington asked.

"I think he will. He doesn't want us telling Dean Messing about his luncheon."

"That luncheon does give him a good motive for killing Teller, and he was sitting there right down the hall when Teller fell. We have proof of that."

I looked at his desk where he had a picture of his wife and daughter and of his son who died in Afghanistan, a daily reminder of how quickly loss can intrude into life.

"I'm not ruling him out, and he's certainly a person with motive. But I think he really believed that Teller was an honorable man and wouldn't reveal his secret to the dean."

"Even to save his job?" Harrington asked. "That's stretching honor pretty far."

"Don't forget there's the practical problem. Despite the fact that he uses a letter opener he claims to have taken away from a mugger, Boyd is about eight inches shorter and fifty pounds lighter than Teller. I'm not sure I can see him pushing the victim out a window."

"He could have taken him by surprise. Or maybe he just snapped and did it in a rage. We both know that when people get worked up their strength can double or triple."

I nodded, having been surprised at how strong weedy little teens could be when they were in a panic. I got to my feet.

"What are you going to do next?" Harrington asked.

"I'm not sure. Guess I'll wait and see if you find Miller."

"If Boyd can give us proof that the kid plagiarized, we'll put out an all points bulletin for him."

"I'll give Boyd until tomorrow afternoon, then lean on him some more."

Harrington nodded. "Let me know when you plan to do that. I'll come along as backup. If he did kill Bianca, we don't want to give him a chance at another victim."

"I think I can handle him."

"Are you even carrying?"

I shook my head.

"Make sure you are while you're on this case. Something is going on here, and I don't like the looks of it."

"Okay, that's probably a good idea. Just because it's a college campus doesn't make it safe."

"At least right now, it's the most dangerous place in town."

Chapter Twenty-Eight

I went back to the office. Right in the center of my desk was the offer the Hastings had made on the house, signed by the owner. They had accepted the offer outright with no counteroffer. Probably they were relieved to have the house off their hands.

"It just came in a few minutes ago. I took it off the fax for you," Nancy said.

"Thanks."

"Congratulations. It looks like you've finally gotten rid of the Hastings."

"I won't count my chickens until the closing is over, but it's a good first step."

I got on the phone and called Roger Hastings. When he answered, sounding preoccupied as usual, I told him the good news, expecting him to sound pleased.

"They didn't argue over the price?" he asked suspiciously.

"No."

"Then I bet we could have gotten the house for even less. Can we lower our offer?"

"You'd be backing out of a signed contract. That might risk your earnest money."

He sighed. "Well, Marcie probably wouldn't go along with negotiating anyway. She pays full price for everything she wants and doesn't think about it."

I kept quiet. I wasn't going to participate in his trashing of his wife.

"What happens now?" he asked.

I described to him the next few steps and the timeline.

"Congratulations!" I said, when I was done, trying to sound upbeat.

"Yeah, yeah," he replied, then hung up without saying goodbye.

Yes, I was definitely not going to miss seeing the last of the Hastings.

Nancy walked over and sat in front of my desk. "I heard a bulletin on the television news at noon that a student was found dead up at Minton State. Does that have anything to do with the story you're working on?"

"Just between us, it does," I said and gave her a summary of the situation.

"That's terrible," she said, shaking her head when I was through. "Young people take such terrible chances. They have no grasp of the consequences of their actions. I know I didn't. When I look back on some of the things I did in my early twenties, I shudder."

"Her main weakness was that she was ambitious. That's generally a good thing, but when it comes to crime, it can get you in a lot of trouble."

"You tried to warn her," Nancy pointed out.

"But I can't shake the feeling that I could have done more. That I didn't use strong enough words to impress upon her the danger she was in."

"Words can only go so far. Short of locking her in a jail cell, I don't think you could have prevented her from getting into trouble."

"Probably not."

"How's Daniel taking it?"

"Not well. He was pretty close to her. I think he feels even guiltier than I do."

"Well, he did encourage her to be an investigative reporter," Nancy said.

"But in a quiet town like Minton, you don't expect it to end this way. You can't really blame Daniel."

"I didn't mean to. But maybe he should have pulled the reins in harder on her."

I shrugged. "It's hard to know how much to discourage a young person from following her dream."

Nancy wasn't saying anything I hadn't told myself and tried to tell Daniel. But now I found myself defending him, whether out of simple loyalty or real belief I wasn't sure. Tired of the conversation and the whole topic of Bianca, I got to my feet. "I think it's time for me to go home. It's been a long day."

I could tell that Nancy regretted having brought up the subject, but I was too tired mentally to spend time making her feel better. With a wave and a good night, I headed out the door.

I was in the car and halfway to my condo when I decided that if I went home now I'd spend hours pacing and stewing. Nervous energy and frustration were a combination unlikely to lead to a relaxing evening. I made a right turn and headed back toward the center of town. Two blocks from the green I pulled into the parking lot for Mike's Fitness Center, housed in a former warehouse not far from the no longer used train station. I always kept a bag with clean workout gear on the back seat, just in case the mood struck me. When I walked in the front door, Mike, a roly-poly fellow who showed no signs of ever using his own equipment, greeted me cordially. I grabbed a protein drink out of the cooler as a substitute for my missed lunch.

"How's it going, Mike?" I asked as I paid.

"Fabulous," he replied, grinning. "The place is crowded today."

I looked along the length of the warehouse and saw that it was indeed bustling with activity. A small group of senior men was seated at the counter in front of Mike. I smiled and they nodded. They always seemed to be sitting there. I frequently wondered if their idea of a workout was to sit at the counter for an hour chatting with Mike, then go home. Perhaps it was somewhere different to go that they were looking for rather than exercise. Of course, maybe a change of scene was good for the brain, which was even more important than using the body.

After gulping the drink I went in the women's locker room and changed. For the next forty-five minutes, I used various aerobic equipment and a number of weight machines, being careful to stretch but not to strain my surgically repaired back. I could feel my mood lighten the more I exerted myself. When I was doing my cool down on the treadmill, I was still thinking about Bianca but with a new emotional distance that didn't cause as much stress. I was paying no attention to my surroundings.

"Hi, there," a voice said from the treadmill next to me.

I glanced over suspiciously. Mike's wasn't the kind of place where on-the-make singles usually hung out. Most of the users were students, serious body builders, or retirees. The man next to me was around thirty and didn't seem to fall into any of those categories. He was tall and slim with brown wavy hair. He gave me a friendly smile. I decided to remain cautious. A lot of men were good actors.

"It's Officer Kate Cameron, isn't it?"

"It used to be. I'm not on the force anymore."

He frowned. "I should have remembered that. I heard around the courthouse a couple of years ago that you took early retirement. I was sorry to learn about your accident."

"Thanks." I studied him. He either knew me or was doing a good job of pretending. He did look vaguely familiar, but I couldn't quite place him."

"You don't remember me, do you?" he asked with a hurt smile.

"I'm afraid not."

"It was quite a while ago, about a year before your accident."

"You seem to be keeping pretty close track of me."

He blushed. "I guess I do. Of course, Minton is a small place, and you are something of a celebrity."

I waved a hand, dismissing the comment.

"Actually, I was the lawyer for the defense in a case where you testified: the Tommy Alvarez case."

Suddenly, it all came back to me. It had been a routine speeding stop, and Alvarez had a bag of cocaine in plain view on the front seat. His lawyer had grilled me for what seemed like hours over whether I could possibly have seen the cocaine on the seat a half hour after twilight. He'd even come up with some bizarre device to test my vision using a shoebox and a flashlight. The judge must have been having a slow day because he went along with all the antics. In the end, I'd passed the test with flying colors, and the prosecution had gotten a conviction.

"You're…" I searched for the name.

"Andrew Harrow," he said, sticking out his hand.

I gave it a quick shake, almost losing my balance on the treadmill.

"I hope you don't harbor a grudge about my behavior in the courtroom."

"Not if you don't harbor a grudge about losing the case."

He laughed. "I never had much of a chance of winning. I was hoping to rattle you and lower your credibility with the jury. Instead, you did fine on my little test, and I just reinforced your testimony. You really made me look foolish, which doesn't happen very often."

"Well, if it's any consolation, I felt pretty foolish myself staring into that shoebox."

"I'm sorry. I was just…"

"Doing my job."

"You've heard it before."

"Frequently, especially from defense lawyers."

"How about from defense lawyers who are asking for a date?"

"Is that what's going on here?" I asked, suddenly cautious again.

"I assume you aren't in law enforcement anymore, so we wouldn't have any conflict of interest."

"I'm in real estate."

He raised an eyebrow, and I noticed that he was—in a way—rather handsome.

"You think that's an odd move from law enforcement?" I asked.

"Not necessarily. But it seems a rather tame

profession for someone like you."

"A wild woman?"

He smiled. "Let's just say you seem to have a certain craving for excitement."

"And would my craving for excitement be satisfied by going out with you?" I asked. I knew I was flirting, but with this guy, it seemed to come naturally.

"I wouldn't want to overpromise, but you could do a lot worse."

He reached into the pocket of his gym shorts and produced a business card, which he handed to me. I felt guilty taking it. However, I was more determined than ever to break it off with Daniel, and this seemed like a way of starting over.

"Can I have your number to give you a call?" he asked.

"I don't carry my business cards with me in the gym although I can see why a lawyer might. In case someone drops a weight on his foot, you can be right on the scene to pick up a client."

He grinned. "Always prepared, just like the scouts."

"Are you prepared enough to have a pen?"

"Sure am." One materialized in his hand. I took the pen and wrote my number on the back of his card. I handed it to him.

"You don't want to keep my card?"

"If you really are interested, give me a call and I'll consider it," I said, stopping the treadmill and stepping off.

"Oh, don't worry, Kate, I'll call," Andrew replied.

"I'm not worried at all," I said, heading toward the locker room.

I didn't turn to look, but I was willing to lay odds that he was watching me as I walked away. I thought about it for a second and decided that I didn't mind at all.

Chapter Twenty-Nine

I had just poured myself a glass of water and was sitting at the kitchen counter wondering what I was going to make for dinner when my cell phone rang. It was my father, a rather rare occurrence since it's usually my mother who calls.

"Is anything wrong?" I asked immediately.

"Why should anything be wrong?"

"You don't usually call."

"Ah, well I was watching the early evening news, and they mentioned that a young woman had been found dead on the campus of Minton State. I wondered if it had anything to do with the case that you're investigating." He paused for a moment. "Your mother is worried that you might be mixed up in something dangerous."

I knew my father well enough to figure that he wouldn't call unless he was concerned as well. Swearing him to secrecy, I gave him an overview of what had happened.

"That's terrible," he said. "And for it to be someone so young with apparently a great deal of talent makes it even worse. Since he worked with her, I'm sure Daniel is devastated."

"Yes, he is." My father had no idea.

"I have every confidence in your abilities, but I hope you are being duly careful in your investigations.

Whoever did this sounds like a dangerous person."

"I'm staying alert."

"Are you making progress in finding the perpetrator?"

"The most I can say now is that we're narrowing down the field."

"Very good. I'm sure it's a slow, methodical process." He paused again, apparently satisfied with my answer. "So I can assume that we'll see you for dinner tomorrow night as usual."

"Of course."

"Just so it doesn't come as a surprise to you, your sister has decided to consider attending a four-year institution. She sprang it on me out of nowhere after stubbornly resisting for some time. I asked her what changed her mind, and she said it was a conversation she'd had with you. Of course, Amanda refused to give me any details. What did you say to her that changed her mind, after I'd argued with her until I was blue in the face?"

I couldn't very well tell him that I'd convinced her that a four-year school would give her more time to get in touch with her sexual identity.

"I eventually got her to understand that modern policing is going to require a bachelor's degree sooner rather than later. Since she's so intent on becoming a cop that seemed to tip the balance for her."

"I see," he said, not sounding truly convinced. "I did try to make that point with her myself, but I'm sure it meant more coming from you."

"Maybe so," I said.

"Well, stay safe, and we'll see you tomorrow."

After I hung up, I opened the slider and went out

on the deck. In the deepening twilight, I could barely see the river, but I heard the water rushing past. I found the sound soothing and tried to let it wash away the bad feelings of the day. I knew the only thing I could do to alleviate my guilt over Bianca's death was to find her killer. Harrington and I seemed to have narrowed it down to Evan Miller and Rockwell Boyd, two men with very different reasons for wanting Joseph Teller dead; both with motive and as far as we knew, opportunity. My intuition told me that it wouldn't be long before we'd gotten it down to just one. I heard my phone buzzing on the kitchen counter and rushed back inside.

"It's me," Daniel announced when I answered.

"How are you doing?"

"How do you think? I spent the better part of the afternoon writing an essentially uninformative article about the murder on campus. It says nothing. Harrington would be very proud of me," he said bitterly.

"You really didn't have any choice."

"Well, I find it demoralizing. It goes against everything I've learned about what journalism is supposed to be. Once you take over the crime beat, I'm going to leave all that sort of thing up to you."

I almost said "thanks" in a sarcastic tone of voice, but restrained myself out of consideration for his depressed mood.

"I spent the rest of the afternoon trying to write Bianca's obituary. I called her parents to see if I could get some personal information and to express my condolences, but they hung up on me."

I was more surprised that he'd be insensitive enough to call them than that they would hang up.

"But I managed to get the information I needed from the funeral home. I'll be running the obituary in tomorrow's paper."

"Fine," I replied, not knowing what else to say.

"The real reason I called is that I was wondering if you'd like to get together for a late dinner. I really don't want to be alone tonight."

The last thing I felt like doing was hand holding with Daniel while he went on about Bianca. But we were still a couple, at least as far as he knew, and I owed it to him. I didn't know when I was going to officially end our relationship, but it would be cruel to add to his emotional burden right now.

"How about I meet you at the River Bend Restaurant in forty-five minutes?" I said. That would give me time for a hot shower and a slow decompression.

"Fine."

When I walked in the lobby of the River Bend a little over forty minutes later, Daniel was already seated at the bar with a martini in front of him. From the awkward way he struggled to his feet and embraced me, I suspected it wasn't his first.

"Are you all right?" I asked.

"Just fine. Just fine," he said with a mirthless grin. "Shall we go in and get a table or would you like to have a drink at the bar?"

I opted for getting a table. Daniel gulped down what was left of his drink, and we walked into the dining room. The hostess led us to a table near the fireplace where a cozy blaze was already going. I took off my coat and sat with my back toward the fire, enjoying the radiating warmth on my stiff muscles. A waitress quickly materialized and asked if we'd like something to drink before dinner.

"I think I'll have another martini," Daniel said quickly.

"I'll have a glass of chardonnay," I said. I looked over at Daniel. "Maybe you should, too?"

An expression of intense thoughtfulness came over his face as if he were seriously considering the idea. "Nope," he said. "I'll have a gin martini."

The waitress wrote down our orders and hurried out to the bar.

"I've been thinking about things," Daniel began, staring intently in my direction. He gave a quick laugh. "I guess people tend to do that when someone close to them dies. It's almost a cliché"

"I suppose so."

"But I have to admit this whole thing with Joe Teller dying and Bianca being killed has really shaken me up."

"That's only natural."

He took an exaggeratedly deep breath. "So I've come to a conclusion, I think it's time for us to live together." His eyes were alive with anticipation as if he expected my face to be immediately wreathed in smiles.

"We've discussed this before," I said in a tone that even to me sounded repressively reasonable. "Your mother would never go along with it."

"I'll take care of that," he said with a grand wave of his arm as if his mother was some minor detail easily overcome, which I knew not to be true.

I wondered whether it was the alcohol or the result of his being on a sort of weird rebound from Bianca that fueled all this bravado. Maybe the sudden death of two people he cared for had made him want to cling more firmly to life and put down roots. Whatever his motivation, I didn't think this was the time to discuss it.

"Maybe we should wait a while before making such a big decision," I said.

He frowned and his lips tightened. "I thought you were all in favor of this."

"I just don't think we should be making any life-altering commitments while you're obviously so upset about Bianca."

The waitress brought our drinks, and we both paused.

"Would you like to order?" she asked.

"Not right now," Daniel snapped.

Realizing something unpleasant was going on, the waitress hurried out of the line of fire.

Daniel took a big sip of his drink. "I'm tired of you implying that my relationship with Bianca was anything but professional. That's an insult to me and to her memory."

I didn't say anything. Now I was getting angry, and I didn't trust myself to speak.

"You were a lot keener on the idea of us living together a few days ago," Daniel said. "What's changed?"

I squirmed in my chair; suddenly the fire behind me seemed oppressively hot.

"I told you before that I don't think now is the right time for this discussion," I said.

He shook his head vehemently. "I think it's the perfect time to get this settled."

I sighed, already regretting what I was going to say.

"I think it's time that we broke things off."

I would have gone on to quickly justify my decision, but I suddenly felt too tired to continue. At first, he smiled as if waiting for the punch line of a not very good joke. Then a look of befuddlement and surprise came over his face, and for a long moment, he seemed unable to speak.

"Is there someone else?" he finally asked.

I shook my head. "I've just come to think that we aren't as suited for each other as I had thought."

"And that's it. You've decided we aren't suited, and you're just going to end it, without talking it over with me or making any effort to work things out."

"I'm afraid that I've made up my mind."

"Well, this is all relatively recent."

I shrugged.

"I'm sure it's all because of Bianca. Just because you were irrationally jealous of her."

I held up my hand. "Stop. I'll leave if you start going down the road of recriminations. I'm not going to sit here while you attack me."

"You'll walk away and leave everything we had behind."

"We had a great six months. We talked about things developing into something more, but neither one of us took any concrete steps to bring that about."

"Now I want to do that and you don't."

"That's about the size of it."

He paused and took a deep breath. "Does this mean that you're going to leave me in the lurch when it comes to *The Sentinel* as well?"

Not having expected to break up with Daniel so soon, I hadn't fully thought through the implications of ending our relationship. But I realized that I liked the idea of being a crime reporter enough to work around any personal awkwardness. I also thought it rather interesting that he had bounced back from romantic rejection to quickly focus on the paper.

"I'll still work on *The Sentinel* if you want me to."

I could see that he was about to shake his head and refuse my offer in a fit of anger when his eyes cleared, and he seemed to suddenly sober up.

"There's no one better suited for the job," he admitted glumly. "We might find it a bit difficult to work together, but I'm sure we're both adult enough to get over it."

I nodded.

"But I'd rather not have dinner with you if you don't mind," Daniel said softly.

"That's fine," I replied, taking my coat off the chair and standing up. He didn't move. "Are you coming with me?"

"I'm going to settle up on the drinks." He smiled. "In fact, I may even have another one—or two."

I stared down at him. "That wouldn't be wise, Daniel, I'm not certain you're fit to drive right now."

"Always the cop," he said with a sneer in his voice.

I bit my tongue. "I can drive you home and bring you back here in the morning to pick up your car."

"Just leave me alone," he said, staring down into his drink. I waited for a moment, but he didn't look up.

"Please be careful," I said and walked away.

I sat in my car in the parking lot for thirty minutes listening to music and wishing I were somewhere else. Finally, Daniel came out and walked over to his car. Fortunately, he didn't look around and see me or else we probably would have had another confrontation. I followed him. He drove with the usual erratic caution of a driver who's had too much to drink, going excessively slow at times then suddenly speeding up. I followed him all the way home and only left when he was parked in the driveway and getting out of his car.

I figured I owed him that much.

As I drove home I went through a kaleidoscope of emotions including anger, guilt, and sorrow. By the time I arrived back at my condo, I realized that my predominant emotion was relief.

Chapter Thirty

I was sitting in my office doing my two-hour stint covering the phones. Although I kept telling myself I should be thinking of creative ways to drum up business, my mind kept going back to Daniel and his suggestion that I was writing off our relationship too soon. It didn't feel that way to me, but maybe he was right and I did tend to walk away from personal relationships when the going got tough. But I couldn't see any sense in making myself miserable by staying with some guy I no longer cared for just to make some point about loyalty. My thoughts jumped back and forth from one side to the other until I was relieved when the telephone rang. It was Detective Harrington.

"We've got Evan Miller," he announced.

"Where did you find him?"

"We didn't. He showed up down at the station a half hour ago with his lawyer. He says he was staying with a cousin of his on campus because he wasn't getting along with his roommate. A student from one of his classes told him that the police had been looking for him, so he called his parents to ask what to do. They got him a lawyer."

"Who's his lawyer?"

"Derrick Hascomb."

"I know him. Doesn't he handle mostly real estate and wills?"

"Yeah, but he knows the boy's father from the Rotary. I guess he plans to take care of things unless it gets serious."

"Does Evan have any idea why you want to question him?" I asked.

"He claims not to. He's doing a good job of looking the picture of innocence. Would you like to sit in on the interrogation?"

"That wouldn't really be appropriate, would it? I'm a civilian—even worse than that I'm a reporter."

"I ran the idea by Evan, and he was thrilled at the idea of having you here. Apparently, you made quite a positive impression on him when you met. Hascomb wasn't too pleased, but eventually, he agreed, as long as you promise not to write about anything you hear in the room."

"But if I found out the same thing through independent sources, I could write about it?"

"You're thinking about getting proof of plagiarism from Rockwell Brody?"

"I'm hoping."

"I don't know why hearing the kid confess to it would prevent you from writing about it if the professor can offer independent proof."

"Good. What time is the interview?" I asked, checking my watch. I saw that I had five more minutes on the phones just as Molly walked in and gave me a wave.

"We're waiting on you," Harrington replied.

"I'll be there in ten minutes." I hung up the phone. "Can you take over five minutes early for me?" I asked Molly.

"Sure. I'm here anyway. Off to a late breakfast

with your boyfriend?"

"Off to the police station."

Molly grinned. "I knew they'd catch up with you some day."

I walked the few blocks to the station at a good clip and easily got there in under the required time. I only had to wait at the front desk for a minute when Harrington came out and waved me in.

"Have you gotten anything out of him?" I asked.

He shook his head. "Once we established that you could be present, he's refused to answer any questions. He just keeps saying 'Let's wait until Ms. Cameron gets here.' You must have made quite an impact on him. I guess you've got a way with younger men."

"I probably remind them of their mothers."

Harrington gave me a long look. "I don't think so," he replied.

We walked down the hall, and he opened the door to an interrogation room. Inside I could see Evan Miller and Attorney Hascomb sitting at the table in the center of the room. They were staring at the walls, apparently having run out of conversation. I doubted they had much in common to chat about in the first place.

"Hi, Ms. Cameron," Evan said with a big smile as I entered the room.

"Hello, Evan." I nodded to Attorney Hascomb who looked even less happy at being here than at a real estate closing.

"Maybe we can begin now," Hascomb said. "I imagine my client has classes, and I certainly have matters to attend to." He turned to me. "I'm sure you're aware that anything said here is to remain out of the newspaper."

I nodded. "Understood."

Harrington cleared his throat and looked down at the manila file open in front of him.

"Evan we're talking to you as part of our investigation into the death of Professor Joseph Teller."

His mouth dropped open in either genuine surprise or a good imitation. "I didn't have anything to do with that. I didn't have any problem with Professor Teller."

"That's not completely true, is it? Didn't the Professor accuse you of having plagiarized a paper you submitted in his journalism class?"

Evan licked his lips. "But I told him that I didn't."

Harrington pushed the plastic evidence bag containing the paper across the table to him. "Is this the paper?"

The boy picked up the bag and after a moment, nodded his head.

"Did you plagiarize this paper?" Harrington asked.

"Don't answer that," Hascomb interjected. "Since when is it the job of the police to investigation the violation of school rules?"

"When the violation of them could be a motive for murder," Harrington snapped.

"But I couldn't have murdered Professor Teller," Evan said.

"Why is that?" I asked softly.

The boy turned to look at me with a pleading expression on his face. "I was in class at the time he died."

"Can you prove that?" Harrington asked.

"I was in Professor Wilson's Survey of British Literature class. He takes careful attendance every day. He'll tell you that I was there."

"He'll be able to swear that you were in class on that day last week?" Harrington asked, sounding incredulous.

"It's a small class—only about twenty—and I've had Professor Wilson before, so he knows me."

"So what about plagiarizing this paper?" Harrington continued, waving the evidence bag at Evan.

"That's irrelevant," Hascomb said. "If Mr. Miller had no opportunity to commit the crime, it doesn't matter whether he had motive or not."

"Evan, I can understand why you might have plagiarized this paper," I said, looking him in the eye. "You told me that you weren't into the gritty side of things, and writing an article like this would have involved asking questions of a stranger. I can see where that might be difficult or embarrassing for you. Maybe you didn't even steal the story from the Internet, but treated it as a creative writing assignment and made up a work of fictional journalism. Even professionals have been known to do that. But telling us whether Teller was right about your story being plagiarized might help us solve his murder."

"That's enough," Hascomb said, standing up. "Unless you are going to charge my client, we are done here."

There was a firmness to his voice and demeanor that I'd never seen before, suggesting that he had hidden skills as a lawyer not revealed during his real estate transactions. Harrington glanced at me, and I gave an almost imperceptible shrug.

"You're free to go, but keep us informed of your whereabouts in case we want to question you further,"

Detective Harrington said.

"Which will only happen when I'm present," Hascomb added. He took Evan by the arm and guided him out of the room. The boy turned to give me a wan smile before the door closed behind him.

"We have to check to see whether he was really in class at the time of Teller's death," Harrington said. "When I went to college, professors were sometimes awfully vague about taking attendance. Sometimes they didn't even know who was supposed to be in the class."

"Yes, we should check on that. But I'd still like to know if Evan plagiarized that paper. If he did steal the story and Teller was going to blow the whistle on him that would be a pretty powerful motive for murder."

"But if he was in class, he couldn't have done it," Harrington pointed out.

"I know. But somehow I still think it might be relevant."

"If you really want to know, you'd better lean harder on Boyd and get him to check that paper. Tell him that if we don't hear from him by tomorrow, I'm going to have another meeting with the dean and who knows what we might discuss. But it will definitely involve that little lunch he had in Northampton."

"I'll give Boyd a call and let him know," I said.

"And I'll set up an appointment for us to meet with this Professor Wilson. I want him to look me in the eye and swear that Miller was in his class that day. Do you want to come along?"

"Sure."

"Good. I'll let you know when I've got it set up."

I paused. "You didn't ask Ethan any questions about Bianca Fitzsimmons. If he killed Teller, don't you think he probably killed Bianca?"

"I do. But we're keeping quiet about Bianca's death being a murder right now. That would be front-page news and bring us a lot of unwanted attention from newspapers all over the state. Plus it might be easier to get Evan to talk about Bianca if we can prove he killed Teller. We have no witnesses or forensics that help us with her death, so there's nothing to use to pressure him. But don't worry, if his alibi doesn't pan out, I'll have him in here again and grill him about Bianca."

"If he does alibi out, I think maybe we should ask around and see if Rockwell Boyd knew Bianca."

Harrington nodded. "Too bad we can't find out who Bianca's secret source was."

"Maybe we should start questioning her friends. She might have mentioned it to one of them."

"We've already talked to her roommate. But she might deserve a second visit. Maybe you could come along. She might be more willing to talk to a woman reporter than to a male cop."

"Arrange it, and I'll be happy to."

When I got back to the office, I called the university switchboard and was connected to Boyd's number. The phone rang several times then switched to voicemail. I left Boyd a pointed message laced with threats that I hoped would prompt him to swiftly check Miller's paper. If it turned out that Evan Miller was innocent that would narrow our suspects down to Boyd himself. I wasn't quite sure how we could get enough proof to make an arrest, but we'd cross that bridge when we came to it.

Molly had left a number on my desk from someone

named Linda McCall who asked that I return her message. I immediately did so, hoping it would be new business.

"Thanks for calling me back," she said. "My husband and I are planning to sell our house and move into a condominium down south, and we were hoping you could handle the sale for us. You were recommended to us by Marcie Hastings."

"Marcie?" For a moment I couldn't believe my ears. Although I had found them the house of their dreams, I still didn't think either one of them liked me much.

"Yes. She said you did a wonderful job finding them a new house."

"That's very gratifying to hear."

We arranged that I would stop tomorrow evening to take a look at their house and work up an asking price. I hung up the phone thinking that this might be my lucky day. My cell phone rang almost as soon as I had hung up the office phone.

"Hi, Kate, it's Andrew Harrow."

"Andrew," I said, surprised.

"You needn't sound so shocked. I promised you I would call."

"Yes…well."

"You didn't think my promise was worth much. Is that because I'm a defense lawyer or because I'm me?"

"More that guys, in general, are always promising to call, and then not following through."

"I don't imagine that happens much to you."

I ignored the compliment. "What did you want to talk about?"

Andrew chuckled. "You don't make it easy, do

you?"

"I've never been big on small talk."

"I was wondering if you'd like to go out for dinner. It would be a chance for us to get to know each other a bit better."

My mind went to work feverishly. Did I want to go out with this guy? He had given me a hard time in the courtroom trying to exonerate his sleazy client. That didn't endear him to me, but it was, after all, what he was paid to do. He did seem smart, and I had to admit he was attractive. Now that I had officially broken things off with Daniel, there was nothing standing in the way of my dating another guy. Still, I wasn't sure I wanted to leap into another relationship quite so soon. The prudent approach would be to take a brief cooling off period to regain my bearings such as they were.

"I was hoping you'd be free on Saturday night, and we could go to the River Bend Inn," he went on a shade nervously after my prolonged silence.

I had inadvertently used the old police trick of staying silent in order to get more out of a suspect. I thought about the possibility of getting the same waitress at the River Bend who had waited on Daniel and me last week. I guess she'd just figure I was a slut. I found I really didn't care. I also figured the hell with prudence. Maybe Mom was right, and it was time for me to get a move on in the relationship department.

"Kate?"

"That would be fine."

"Good," he said, the relief evident in his voice. "Shall I pick you up?"

"Why don't we meet at the restaurant?" Over the years I had become cautious about giving directions to my home, although anyone with some technical savvy could probably find my location via the Internet. There was no such thing as real privacy anymore.

"Okay. Shall we say at seven o'clock?"

I agreed. Generally, I liked eating earlier, but I'd need time to get ready for a date after getting home from work. I was manning the phone Saturday afternoon.

"That will be fine."

"I'm looking forward to it," Andrew said enthusiastically.

"So am I," I replied in what I knew was a less than spirited tone.

After I cut the connection, I sat there for a moment wondering why I had such mixed feelings about my date with Andrew. True, he was a hard-driving defense lawyer and might be a poor fit for my law and order mindset, but I'd dated guys before who didn't share my viewpoint on everything. Usually, I liked arguing with someone who had a different point of view, especially if he could offer good reasons for his position. Some of the best conversations Daniel and I had had were over the importance of freedom of the press versus privacy rights. We may have gotten heated, but we never lost respect for each other.

Thinking about those times with Daniel brought back in a rush all the good times we had spent together. And I recalled how anxious I had been for us to start living together and how frustrated I had become as that time got pushed further and further off into the future because of his unwillingness to confront his mother. Now that I thought about it, I realized that his inability to make a firm decision had slowly undermined my confidence in him. Even if Bianca had never happened along, I doubted that our relationship would have lasted beyond a couple of months.

By the time he had finally decided that we should live together, I had on some deep level decided that I didn't really want to. How long I would have hidden that from myself, I wasn't sure. Maybe my desire to start living a more stable life, with a solid relationship at the center of it, would have blinded me to my doubts. We might even have moved in together before I became aware of my mistake.

The more I thought about it, the more I realized that Bianca had unknowingly done me a favor by causing me to question my confidence in Daniel. I felt I owed her something in return—finding her murderer.

Chapter Thirty-One

"So we're going to check out Boston University, Northeastern, and UMass Boston," my father said, checking them off on his fingers. "A good university will offer Amanda more options if she changes her mind and decides that she really doesn't want to go into criminal justice."

"I won't change my mind," Amanda said.

"That's what you think now. But you really don't know anything about what the study of criminal justice entails. Once you get into it, you might find that it isn't challenging enough intellectually," Dad said in his most reasonable teacher's voice that drove Amanda and me crazy.

"You mean I might decide to switch to science or math," Amanda said. "You'd like that wouldn't you?"

"Those are your strengths," Dad replied.

Amanda glanced at me and rolled her eyes.

"Or you could study computer science," Mom put in. "Joan Carter's nephew majored in that, and he's earning fifty thousand in his first year out of college."

"I'd rather cut my throat with a broken bottle," Amanda said.

"Amanda!" Mom shouted.

"You have to stay open to possibilities," Dad said. He turned to me. "Don't you agree?"

"I think there are real advantages to a large

university. There's a greater variety of people and being in Boston means a more diverse social scene," I said.

Amanda smiled at me, and I saw a calculating gleam in her eye.

"Well, those three schools would certainly be a place to start," she said, suddenly more amenable.

Dad gave her a keen look as if wondering exactly what was going on. He suspected something but couldn't put his finger on it. He glanced over at me, but I kept my expression neutral.

"I'm not so sure about Boston," Mom said. "It's a large city. Will Amanda be safe?"

"I'll be fine, Mom," Amanda said.

My mother shook her head, unconvinced.

"A city will give her more cultural opportunities," Dad continued, ever the teacher. "Sometimes you learn as much from your environment as you do in class."

Amanda smiled, and I thought I knew what was going through her mind. The learning she had in mind was definitely not going to go on in class.

"How is Daniel?" Mom asked.

"He's fine." I almost left it at that, not being anxious to reveal my break with Daniel to my family. But then I realized that I had to tell them eventually and waiting would just make it worse. "Actually we've broken up."

"Why, Kate?" Mom said plaintively. "He's such a nice boy."

"Things just weren't going the way I had expected."

I looked across the table and caught Amanda's eye. She was studying me carefully as if trying to figure out the true meaning behind my words.

"Sometimes you've got to be willing to compromise, Kate. Everything isn't always going to go your own way," Mom said. She looked down at my father's end of the table, her eyes imploring him to come to her support.

My father cleared his throat. "I'm certain Kate knows what she's doing," he said reluctantly.

"Well, I'm not sure she does. Why don't any of her relationships seem to last longer than six months?" Mom asked.

"Maybe she's just particular," Amanda said.

I gave her a grateful glance.

"There's such a thing as being too fussy," Mom shot back. "None of us are perfect, after all."

"I'm sure Kate is aware of that," Dad said. "And after all, she's the one who has to be happy with the man, not you."

Mom glared at him as if not at all sure at the moment that *she* had made the right choice in men. Finally, she sighed and tears filled her eyes.

"I just keep hoping that someday you'll settle down. I don't want you to be alone after your father and I are gone."

"That won't be for a long time. And she'll always have George and me," Amanda said.

"George has a wife and family, and someday you'll settle down with a husband and have a family of your own."

Amanda gave me a mischievous look.

"Neither of you will have much time for your spinster sister," Mom continued.

I reached over and touched her hand. "Don't worry, Mom, I'm sure that I'll settle down—some day."

Mom gave me a faint smile and wiped at her tears.

"How are you coming along in your investigation into the death of Joseph Teller?" Dad asked neatly changing the subject.

"We've narrowed down our list of suspects to two and are hoping to gather enough evidence to decide which of them did it."

"Will you have enough to bring charges?" Dad asked.

"It's too soon to tell. I certainly hope so."

"And what about that poor girl who was killed— the one who worked on *The Sentinel*. Have you found out any more about what happened to her?" asked Mom.

"Since she was investigating Teller's death, we think it's all somehow connected. She probably got too close to the killer or threatened to expose him."

"All this makes me glad you aren't in police work anymore," Mom said.

I paused for a moment, uncertain whether to tell them the rest of the truth about Daniel and myself. Finally, I decided that they'd be seeing my name in *The Sentinel* soon enough, so it was better to tell them now.

"Actually, I'm taking over the job Bianca had as crime reporter."

"But you've got a job already," Mom objected.

"Daniel needed somebody to take over for Bianca and offered me the job. I don't know how long I'm going to stay with it, but I feel that I sort of owe it to him."

"A consolation prize for dumping him," Amanda said, grinning.

I glared at her. "I wouldn't exactly put it that way."

"But won't working together be a bit difficult under the circumstances?" Dad said.

"I suppose so, but Daniel and I are both professionals in our own ways. We want this to work, so we'll make adjustments."

"Like you should have done in your relationship," Mom added.

I didn't say anything. She was hitting on a sensitive point because I half-felt that she might be right, although I seriously doubted whether we could have worked things out no matter what adjustments we made. My father looked at me, and I could tell he realized that I was close to becoming upset.

He clapped his hands together and smiled. "Let's move on to dessert," he said with even more enthusiasm than usual.

Chapter Thirty-Two

I was sitting at my kitchen counter reading the newspaper and having my cereal and coffee. I'd had a good morning run and was feeling both relaxed and virtuous. Since I'd already looked up directions to the McCalls, the folks I was going to be visiting tonight to appraise their home, I didn't have much on my real estate work agenda for today. However, before I could experience much sense of leisure my phone rang.

"Are you ready to start work as a reporter?" Daniel asked without preliminaries.

From the coolness of his tone I figured he thought the best way of handling our break up was to ignore that it had ever happened.

"Sure."

"Then I'll give your name and number to Sergeant Jackson. He's the public affairs liaison for the department. He'll let you know when there's been some event that you might want to report. He'll give you the details from the police report. Once in a while, you might have to do a little research, but most of the time he can tell you all you need to know."

"I don't actually have to be at the point of the incident?"

"Were you going to sit with a police scanner by your desk all day and rush out to crime scenes?" he asked.

I detected a note of sarcasm in his voice that I didn't care for but decided not to call him on it.

"Jackson will tell me whenever there's something worth reporting? He's a crony of the chief. Are you sure he's really going to get in touch with me?"

"He'll call you. There's nothing the department likes better than making front-page news with a drug bust or making a domestic violence arrest. It shows the public that the police are doing their job."

"What do I do once I've written up the story?"

"You send it to the paper via e-mail. Myra can show you how to do that. I take a look at it, do whatever editing needs to be done, and send it on to production. Next thing you know, you'll see your name in print. You'll get paid thirty-five dollars a story. Myra will keep track of how many you submit and send you a check at the end of each month."

I realized with something of a shock that I'd never have to see Daniel as part of the job. Somehow that made our break seem all the more final.

"Are those terms all right with you?" he asked.

"Sounds fine," I said, imitating his clipped tones. I wanted to say I was sorry for the way things had worked out, but I didn't think he'd appreciate the apology. Clearly, putting up an emotional wall was his way of dealing with this, and any attempt to break through would merely make him angry.

"Okay. Then I look forward to our having a good professional relationship," he said with a hint of irony.

"So do I."

He waited for a moment as if expecting me to say more.

"Thanks for everything," I finally replied and hung

up.

I sat at the counter, staring at my soggy cereal. So this was the way it was going to end, not with a friendly kiss or even handshake, but with hurt feelings and silent recriminations. We were going from lovers to business acquaintances, and not very friendly ones at that. Well, we were both getting what we wanted. He was getting a police reporter with some field experience, and I was getting a chance to dabble in crime. We'd just have to see how it all worked out.

My cell phone rang again, and this time it was Detective Harrington.

"I've arranged a meeting with Stanley Wilson, Evan Miller's British literature professor. The one who can supposedly vouch for him being in class at the time of Teller's murder."

"When are you meeting with him?"

"Nine o'clock at his office. It's right down the hall from the English Department. Can you meet me there?"

"Sure."

"I also got in touch with Bianca Fitzsimmons' roommate. The officer who interviewed her the first time didn't ask her anything about Bianca's friends, just whether she had any enemies. If we talk to her friends we might get a better idea of who she was spending time with shortly before her death."

"Good idea."

I showered quickly and put on one of my business casual real estate broker's outfits. I'd look professional, but not stand out too much on campus. Keeping my word to Harrington, I did strap on my Glock under my jacket just to be careful. As I drove to the university, I wondered what we were going to do if it turned out that

Evan Miller did have a solid alibi for Teller's death. That would leave only Rockwell Boyd as a suspect. He certainly had opportunity, being only a few yards away at the time of Teller's death. He also had motive since Teller could easily have informed Dean Messing about his other boyfriend. Whether he had means depended on whether you thought he was strong enough to push the larger man out the window. Finding evidence placing him in the office at the time of death would be difficult. But I made a note to myself to ask Harrington to check with forensics. If we could find a fingerprint from Boyd on the window frame, that might lend support to the theory of his guilt. Boyd could always argue that he had been in the office before, so his prints would be there. But prints on the windowsill would be harder to ignore.

When I got to the English Department office, Harrington was already there. I nodded to Janet Phillips, who flashed me a brief smile. Fiona Halsey, the student intern, raised her head and gave me a long searching look.

"We're just going down the hall to talk with Professor Wilson, he's expecting us," Harrington said.

Janet Phillips had a puzzled expression as if wondering why we were meeting with Professor Wilson, but all she said was, "His office is down three doors on the left."

Harrington nodded and thanked her. His office turned out to be very close to Rockwell Boyd's, which was a little farther up on the other side. I commented on that to Harrington.

"Too bad Wilson wasn't here when Teller was murdered, he might have been able to give us something," he replied.

We knocked on the door and received a call to enter. The man standing behind the desk didn't fit my stereotyped idea of an English professor as someone with longish hair, a bent frame, and a ravaged face. That was the way most of mine had looked. This guy had short gray hair, was about my height, and had the wiry build of someone who stayed in condition. He came around the desk and greeted each of us with a firm handshake. He motioned for us to sit down, and I noticed that, unlike Rockwell Boyd's office, all the surfaces were clear of papers and books. Here was an organized man. He sat across from us and frowned.

"When you said on the phone that you wanted to talk to me about Evan Miller, I have to admit that I was surprised. Evan is the last person I'd expect to be involved in a police matter. He's a very serious, conscientious student who seems completely devoted to his studies."

Harrington took out his notebook and read out the date of Teller's murder. "We'd really like to know if Miller was in your British Literature class that day."

"I can tell you without even checking my records that Evan was in class. He hadn't been absent at all this semester until earlier this week."

"You know that off the top of your head?" I said.

He nodded. "First of all, it is a small class, only fifteen students, so I can easily keep track of who is present. Secondly, Evan is very active in terms of participation. I'd have missed him if he weren't there. I can assure you that the class doesn't go nearly as well without Evan there to answer the more difficult questions."

"I understand," Harrington said, "but I'd have more confidence in your testimony if you had some kind of paper record to support it."

Wilson nodded. "I can supply that. He got up and took a manila folder off his desk. He pulled out a spreadsheet. "This is the attendance record for that class," he said, holding it so we both could see. "You'll notice the names of the students go down the lefthand side and across the top are the dates of every class. There is a square for each student for every class. I put an "A" or "P" in that square to indicate whether the student was absent or present on that day. You'll see that for the date you asked about there is a "P" in Evan's square, so he definitely was there."

"That's a very meticulous system for taking attendance," I said. "Are most faculty so careful?"

Wilson laughed. "It varies. Some have no idea of who's in their classes at all. They couldn't match a name with a face even at the end of the semester. Others keep some kind of record of attendance, but it may be rather spotty. Many years ago I taught at West Point where you were ordered to keep accurate attendance records and had to turn them in at the end of every week. This is pretty much the West Point method, and it's served me well over the years. Also, occasionally a student will challenge me when I deduct some points for poor attendance, so it's always good to have an accurate record."

"Well, thank you for your help," Harrington said, starting to stand.

Wilson stood as well and faced us. "The only event that occurred that day that I can imagine warranting a police investigation is the death of Joseph Teller. Do your questions have something to do with that?"

"I'm afraid that we really can't talk about an ongoing investigation," Harrington said.

"I understand. It was foolish of me to ask." He paused for a moment. "All the same I'd be very surprised if Evan got himself involved in anything as serious as that."

As we walked down the hall, Harrington said, "I guess that takes Evan Miller off our list of suspects. If he was in class, he couldn't have been killing Teller."

"I'd still like to know if he plagiarized that story," I said.

"What difference does it make now?"

"It would give him a motive."

Harrington glanced at me shrewdly. "You think he got someone else to do it."

I shrugged.

"Have you heard back from Boyd on whether he checked on Miller's paper?"

"I left him a voicemail strongly encouraging him to do so, but he hasn't gotten back to me. I think he's afraid of getting involved in a lawsuit."

"I'll give him a call this afternoon and point out the benefits of cooperating to him. Although whatever he decides to do, I guess we have to focus our attention on him. He's the only suspect left."

"Thinking about that, I was wondering whether it might not be a good idea to get a set of his fingerprints. We could check them against those found in Teller's office." I told him my idea of trying to find one in an incriminating spot.

"Good idea. The problem is he may not agree to be printed. Let me think about it, maybe I can come up with a way to get his prints without going the formal route."

"I wonder if we could get Boyd to confess. If it turns out that Evan did plagiarize, I could tell Boyd that his student is our primary suspect. He doesn't have to know that Evan has a solid alibi for the time of the murder."

"You think Boyd would confess rather than see his student take the fall?"

I shrugged. "I don't know."

"I think you might be giving the professor too much credit for having a conscience."

Harrington pointed toward a large institutional building in the distance.

"That was Bianca's dorm. Let's go have a chat with her roommate."

Once again, the student on door duty started to interrogate us, but he, too, seemed appropriately intimidated by Harrington's badge and let us pass.

"I wonder, would he know a real badge from a phony one?" Harrington asked.

"Maybe they need a little more training. He should at least have written down your name and badge number."

We went up to the fourth floor and knocked on the door.

"I called ahead," Harrington said softly. "I didn't want to frighten her."

A willowy girl with long brown hair opened the door and stared at us. She twisted her long fingers anxiously.

"Are you the police?"

"I am," Harrington said, showing his badge. "Ms.

Cameron is assisting me. Are you Meghan Green?"

She nodded.

"May we come in and talk with you for a moment?" Harrington asked.

Meghan stepped out of the doorway, and we moved into the room. It was somewhat larger than Evan's and more nicely decorated on what I took to be Meghan's side of the room. The other side was stripped down. Apparently, Bianca's personal items already had been removed.

Meghan saw me looking. "Bianca's parents came and took everything away this morning." She looked like she was about to cry. "Now it really feels like she's gone.

"You and Bianca were good friends?" I asked.

"We've roomed together since sophomore year." She paused and her lower lip trembled. "I don't know how I'm going to get along without her. I discussed everything with her. She helped me make decisions."

I could easily imagine Bianca making decisions for this shy, diffident young woman.

"Did you see Bianca on the day she returned from the hospital?" Harrington asked.

Meghan shook her head. "Her parents brought her here from the hospital in the afternoon. I had class from noon until four. Then I ate in the dining room, and I had a three-hour lab after that. When I got back around nine, I found her."

She began to sway. Harrington reached out and grabbed her arm, easing her down on the bed.

"Are you going to be okay?" he asked.

"I just can't believe this is happening," she said as tears began running down her cheeks.

I sat on the bed next to her and took her hand. "I'm sure it was an awful shock finding Bianca that way."

"At first I thought she was sleeping, but she was so still I got worried. I tried to wake her up, and when I couldn't I called security. I thought maybe she had suffered some kind of a stroke from her injury. Is that what happened?"

"We don't know yet," I said soothingly.

"Where was her pillow?" asked Harrington.

"Under her head," she answered with a puzzled expression. The police obviously hadn't told her that Bianca had been killed let alone smothered.

"Did Bianca talk much about her work on *The Sentinel*?" I asked.

"She talked a lot about her boss. She said he was a real hottie."

I saw a smile pull at the corners of Harrington's mouth and frowned.

"What about the work she did there?" I continued.

"I knew she was writing a newspaper story about Professor Teller's death."

"Did she say anything about it?" Harrington asked.

Meghan shook her head. "I'm a social work major. She knew I wasn't very interested in journalism. I didn't even like the idea of Bianca doing it. I told her that going around accusing people of things would only get her into trouble." She looked off across the room as if imagining Bianca still being there. "She was much more daring than I was. She said that I was a lot like a second mother, the way I was always warning her not to do risky things."

"Did she have any other close friends?" I asked.

Meghan paused, as if reluctant to admit that Bianca

had had any friends other than herself. "She was friendly with some of the other English majors."

"Anyone in particular?" I asked.

"I didn't really pay attention to their names," she replied.

I didn't believe that. Anyone as possessive as Meghan probably had memorized the names of everyone Bianca mentioned even in passing.

"This might help us to find Bianca's killer," I reminded her.

She frowned. "Well, there is Lydia Bancroft. She's right down the hall. Bianca used to spend quite a bit of time in her room sometimes. They were in a lot of classes together," she said as if that explained the attraction.

"Did Bianca mention anyone in particular who was giving her help with the Teller investigation?" Harrington asked.

"She said that there was a person who told her about the connection between Professor Boyd and Dean Messing. You already knew about that, right?" she asked, blushing slightly.

We nodded.

"That's when I told her to leave the Teller case alone. I warned her that getting involved with the faculty and staff would lead to nothing but trouble."

"But she didn't listen?" Harrington said.

"She was too excited. She said this was a scandal that would break the university wide open. She thought it would get her a job on a real newspaper."

I didn't think Daniel would be happy to hear that comment.

"Did she tell you the name of the person who gave

her the information about Messing and Boyd?" I asked.

"No."

"Did you ask?"

"Actually, I did. She made such a big deal about it that I got curious. But Bianca said she couldn't share that, even with me. She had promised to keep the name confidential, and a good reporter didn't reveal confidential sources. That's what she said."

At least Bianca was consistently tight-lipped, an admirable trait in some ways but one that had gotten her killed.

"Is there anything else you can tell us that might be helpful?" Harrington asked.

"No. I visited her in the hospital once just before she left that morning and told her to listen to her parents and forget about this journalism thing. She said she would. She said she was thinking about going into television news reporting instead. But somehow I didn't think she was ready to let go of the story she was working on."

"You think she had a new lead?" Harrington asked.

Meghan nodded. "She had that excited look she got when things were going right for her." The girl paused. "But I guess things didn't go right for her at all."

****

"Too bad Bianca was so secretive," Harrington whispered to me as we walked down the hall.

"Having secrets gave her power over other people. That's what she craved. If she hadn't been a journalist, she'd have made an excellent blackmailer."

"You just didn't like her."

"True. But that doesn't make me wrong."

We knocked on Lydia's door and got no answer.

We were about to leave when a young woman came rushing down the hall carrying a basket of laundry. She was short but moved along with an energetic stride.

"Are you looking for me?" she asked, giving us a toothy smile.

"Are you Lydia?" Harrington asked.

"Sure am."

Harrington went through the routine of identifying us.

"I suppose you're here to talk about Bianca," Lydia said over her shoulder as she opened the door to her room with a key attached to a lanyard.

"Why would you suppose that?" I asked with a smile.

"Because I was her best friend."

"I thought Meghan was her best friend," I said, once we had stepped into the room.

Her mouth twisted. "She *wanted to be* Bianca's best friend, but actually she was her slave. Whenever Bianca wanted an errand run, she would get Meghan to do it. It wasn't always very pretty. Bianca really knew how to boss folks around."

"But she was still your best friend?" I asked, amazed at her low standards for friends.

"No friend is perfect."

"Did Bianca talk to you about her investigation into the death of Professor Teller?" Harrington asked.

"Sure. She told me all about the dean and Professor Boyd. That was certainly weird. I couldn't believe they were going to cheat Professor Teller out of his job like that."

Bianca apparently hadn't been shy about sharing information with her self-appointed best friend.

"Did she tell you where she got that information from?" Harrington asked.

"She wouldn't give me the person's name. I couldn't believe it. She told me pretty much everything. But she got uppity when I asked her. Like I was demanding that she break some kind of an oath."

"Did she give you any hints as to who it was?" I asked.

"All she would tell me is that it was someone in the English Department."

"Did she mean faculty, staff, or a student?" I pressed.

"I asked her the same thing. She told me she couldn't answer that question. It would give too much away."

"'Couldn't' or 'wouldn't'?" asked Harrington.

"I think she said she couldn't. I asked her why and she said it wasn't that easy to explain."

"When did you have this conversation with her?" I asked.

"Before she was attacked."

"Did you visit her in the hospital?"

Lydia shook her head. "I meant to, but I got awfully busy."

"You didn't happen to see her the day she came back from the hospital?"

"No. She called me from the hospital and said she was returning to campus around noon, but she had things to do in the afternoon. We were going to get together in my room that evening, but she never showed up. Then I heard the commotion out in the hall when security and the EMTs arrived and found out that she was dead. What caused it? Was it the blow to her head?

Did she have some sort of internal bleeding?"

"We're not sure yet," Harrington lied.

He'd managed to keep a tight lid on things so far. Only Bianca's parents and Daniel knew that she had been murdered. I figured the silence couldn't last more than a few days. Once the autopsy report was out, the state boys would want to get involved since it was a clear case of murder, not just a possible murder as in the case of Teller. That would get the Boston papers on the scene. A college girl murdered on campus would be sensational news. I figured Harrington or maybe the chief would have to meet with the university president soon to discuss the situation. The clock was definitely ticking.

"Is there anyone else that Bianca might have confided in?" I asked.

"Bianca knew a lot of people."

"She was a real extrovert?" I asked.

"It was more that she liked to gossip or at least get other people to gossip with her. She always said that you have to tell a little to get a lot. Finding out things was what Bianca was all about. She'd get this important look on her face sometimes and say, 'Information is power.' I guess she'd heard it somewhere."

"But you can't think of anyone she would have told about her confidential source?" Harrington asked.

Lydia shook her head. "Like I said, I was her best friend. If she didn't tell me, she didn't tell anyone."

We thanked her and Harrington gave her his card with instructions to call him if she thought of any new information.

"So that was Bianca's best friend," Harrington mused as we walked down the hall. "She didn't seem too broken up about Bianca's death."

"We get the friends we deserve," I said.

"From what we're learning about Bianca, perhaps you're right."

I had turned off my phone while we were conducting our interviews. When I switched it back on, I saw that I had a voicemail. I listened to it as Harrington and I walked across campus.

"That was Professor Boyd," I told Harrington. "He's agreed to check out Evan Martin's paper. He needs to arrange to get the software from the department put on his office computer. Since he doesn't have an e-mail copy of the paper, he'll have to scan it. All that's to say that he probably won't have a determination until tomorrow afternoon. He wants me to come see him during his office hour at two o'clock."

"Maybe we should have him come down to the station. We can get him to give us his fingerprints at the same time."

"If he agrees. Like you said yesterday, you don't have enough to arrest him and force him to give us his prints. And if you try to pressure him to comply, he may not tell us about the paper."

"Okay," Harrington said, frowning. "First things first. We find out if Evan plagiarized, then we try to convince Boyd to give us his prints for elimination purposes. If the kid didn't plagiarize, he's definitely off the hook. Then we focus on the professor."

"Sounds like a plan."

"Let's hope something shakes loose before Bianca Fitzsimmons' death goes public. The chief will have my head if we don't catch a break before that. "

I knew he was right and didn't envy him.

Chapter Thirty-Three

I went back to the office and ate a tuna sandwich I had brought from home. I washed it down with some bitter office coffee that had probably been on the burner since nine. I figured that at least it would help keep me awake. Sandy, one of the new realtors in the company that I didn't know well, finished up her phone coverage at noon, and I took over for the next two hours. Usually, I read when there's nothing else to do. There are few things more boring than staring at the phone waiting for it to ring. But today the book sat open on my desk, while I stared across the street at the town green mulling over the morning's interviews.

The more I thought about it, the more I was convinced that Bianca's source couldn't have been another student. What was the likelihood that a student would know about the relationship between Messing and Boyd? Unless someone happened upon them sharing an intimate moment on campus, it was extremely unlikely, and I doubted that they were foolish enough to do that. That left the faculty and staff. Jessica Franks, the department chair, definitely knew about the relationship, but why would she share the information with Bianca? All I could think of was the somewhat farfetched theory that she wanted to protect Teller's job or really wanted to get rid of Boyd, Messing or both. My impression of her was that she was cautious, good at university politics, and not likely to make waves unless it was absolutely necessary.

Of course, lots of other faculty might have had the information. If Franks knew, others in the English Department might have been privy to the story. But would any of them have shared it with Bianca, who had a campus reputation as being impetuous and was known to work for *The Sentinel*? Maybe that was why the source had sworn her to secrecy. It could be a faculty member who had a grudge against the dean or Rockwell Boyd. But interrogating every member of the faculty was impossible. Even questioning every member of the English Department was a daunting task. Especially since it was unlikely that the culprit would admit his or her involvement.

What about staff? Janet Phillips struck me as someone who probably knew as much about the Department as any faculty member, and she gave off vibes that suggested she wasn't a big fan of Professor Boyd's. However, her motherly attitude toward students made it unlikely she would share sensitive information with them, and she was well aware of Bianca's tendency to sensationalize a story. I sat back in my chair, not sure how to proceed.

When my phone time was just about up, Nancy came in to take over.

"How're you doing?" she asked.

I shrugged. "Pretty good."

Nancy paused. "Look, I'm sorry about last time. I didn't mean to make you feel like you were responsible in any way for that girl's death. There was nothing you could have done to stop her from pursuing that story."

"That doesn't seem to prevent me from feeling

guilty. She was a stubborn, headstrong, manipulative young woman, but we all make mistakes when we're young. She shouldn't have had to die for them."

"That's why you're trying to find who killed her. That's the most you can do. Are you and Daniel still working together on that story?"

"I guess so."

Nancy raised an eyebrow.

"Well, I'm still working on the case, and now I'm the crime reporter for *The Sentinel*. But how much we're working together remains to be seen. We've broken up as a couple."

"Because of this girl?"

"Partly, I feel he shouldn't have been so gullible, so easily taken in by her. If he was so unaware, I wondered whether I could I really trust him to make the right choices in the future. Although now that I think about it, I've had doubts about where we were going for quite a while." I sighed, not fully able to explain. "There were a lot of different reasons."

"There always are. Couples never split up for just one reason—even if that's what they think. It's an accumulation of things wearing down the relationship over time."

"If that's true, then Bianca was just the final blow that caused everything to collapse."

"This girl sounds like she was very clever at knowing how to find people's weaknesses."

"That was certainly true with Daniel. She knew he was most proud of being a journalist, and that's how she played up to him."

"You don't think she was serious about wanting to write for the paper."

233

"I think she liked seeing her name in print and enjoyed nosing into other people's business. But probably the prime reason for her interest in journalism was to get close to Daniel. He had a real blind spot when it came to her."

The phone rang and Nancy rushed over to answer it. I packed my things together and gave her a wave as I went out the door. As I got in my car, I decided to stop in the gym on my way home. I had called Sergeant Jackson to see if there were any stories for me to work on for tomorrow's paper, but it seemed that crime—at least interesting crime—had taken a holiday in Minton, so the rest of my day was free until my meeting with my clients tonight.

After a hello to Mike and a nod to the assorted seniors gathered around his counter, I did my usual workout. My thoughts were divided between my upcoming date with Andrew Harrow and my discussion with Nancy about why Daniel and I had split up. I found myself wondering if I would have been quite so definite with Daniel if I didn't already have Andrew waiting in the wings. The thought that this might be true didn't make me feel very good about myself. Like Nancy had said, there were lots of different factors involved in people splitting up, and some of them might not be very attractive. I knew, deny it as he may, Daniel still had strong feelings for Bianca. I could still picture the devastated expression on his face when he told Harrington and me that Bianca had hung up on him at the end of their last conversation.

A question suddenly occurred to me, and I stepped off the treadmill. I found a quiet corner of the gym and called Daniel on my cell phone. He didn't seem happy to hear from me.

"You told Harrington and me that you spoke to Bianca on the day she left the hospital, is that right?"

"Yes, in the morning."

"That was after I had filled you in on how our investigation was progressing. Did you tell Bianca about the Evan Miller plagiarism matter?"

There was a long pause. "I summarized the status of the investigation for her. She asked, and I felt that as a member of the team she had a right to know."

"So you did tell her about Evan Miller?"

"Yes."

I wanted to shout; *Didn't you think that was like pouring kerosene on her ambitions? Couldn't you predict that going to see Evan would be the next thing she'd do?*

But I didn't say anything. Instead, I took a deep breath.

"I did warn her not to continue on the story," Daniel said weakly. Even he was beginning to see his mistake.

"I'm sure you did," I said. "I'm sure you did."

As soon as I was off the phone with Daniel, I called Harrington and told him about Daniel's conversation with Bianca.

"That was stupid," he said flatly.

"Daniel never did think clearly when it came to Bianca," I said.

"I'm going to call Attorney Hascomb right away. I want to set up another interview with Miller. This time we'll ask him about Bianca. Probably the soonest I can get it set up is for tomorrow morning. I'll give you a call."

Glen Ebisch

* * * *

In the evening I drove up from the Minton Valley to the McCalls' house. They were in a development on a set of hills that overlooked the town. They had a nice location on a cul-de-sac that afforded them a good view to the west. On a clear day, you could see out to the middle of the Berkshires. The woman who opened the door was short and somewhat plump. She said she was Linda McCall. Linda had a friendly face and a rapid stream of small talk about how happy she was that I had taken on the selling of their house. She took me through to a family room in the back where a tall, serious looking man came over and shook my hand and introduced himself as Sam McCall. Over his shoulder, I could see that the room had large windows looking out to the west. All the trees and foliage had been cleared away, so you had a direct view of the hills.

"I'm afraid you're about a half hour too late to see the sunset. It was spectacular tonight," he commented.

"A location like this will make your house easy to sell. Why do you want to leave?"

"We're both retiring in January, and we want to live closer to our children in North Carolina. We're having a house built down there," Linda said.

"When will it be finished?"

"In another month," her husband said. "We wanted to have it done in advance in case this house sells quickly. That way we can move our stuff in down there and just rent up here for a few months until the end of the year."

"And you chose me to represent you because you know Marcie Hastings?" I asked.

"I don't really know her well. I had her as a student

a number of years ago," Linda said, "and I see her around town. I'd heard she was looking for a new house, so when I ran into her the other day, I asked if she'd be interested in ours. That's when she told me that you'd already found her the ideal place. I knew you must be good because Marcie isn't easy to please, and from what I've heard, neither is her husband."

I kept a studiously neutral expression. "It took a little bit of looking, but we finally found a place they both liked."

"But Marcie wasn't the only reason we got in touch with you. I teach at the high school, and I know your father. He's a great guy and a wonderful teacher."

"He certainly is," I said.

"We also remember when you saved all those people over in the library," Sam said softly. "We thought that anyone who could do that had to have something on the ball."

I smiled and tried to look modest. I thought Maggie would be delighted that hiring a local celebrity was paying off.

"As you may know," Linda said, "Sam is a family doctor in town, and some of those folks in the library were patients of his."

"I thought your name sounded familiar. I'm sure your leaving town will be a great loss to the community," I said.

He shook his head. "The practice of medicine isn't what it once was. It's better that I leave it to the younger folks. I'm sure they'll do a fine job."

"Sam just lost one of his patients recently, a real tragedy. It was Professor Teller, the man who died on the Minton University campus. It's really a shame when someone around our age—which isn't really that old today—dies in a freak accident. He was healthy enough to live another twenty years."

"Linda—"

"Well, it's true, and I'm not saying anything confidential."

"Have the police been in touch with you about Professor Teller's health? I know from my time on the force that they usually would be."

"Yes. They contacted me to ask my opinion of his state of mind and general health," Sam admitted.

"Did you tell them about his arthritic knees?" Linda asked.

He shot her a sharp glance no doubt meant to silence her, but she was having none of it.

"Well, didn't you say that he needed to have those knees replaced?"

"He wasn't exactly tottering around, but they gave him some pain. And he wasn't as steady on his feet as he might have been because of them. But I doubt he went out a window because of bad knees," Sam said.

"All the same," I said, trying not to be too pushy, "you might want to let the police know. Detective Harrington is on the case. He's a good man, and I'm sure he'd like to know every detail."

The doctor stared at the carpet for a moment. "Okay, maybe you have a point. It's probably won't make any difference, but the police should have all the facts."

I nodded and wondered whether having bad knees would be enough to allow a small man like Rockwell Boyd to push a bigger man such as Joe Teller out a window. I knew Harrington would soon be wondering the same thing.

An hour and a half later, I finally left the house, having had the complete tour, coffee and cake, and established a price that would give me a tidy commission if it sold. But most importantly, I had another lead in the case.

Chapter Thirty-Four

I was sitting at my kitchen counter having breakfast and working on a classified ad describing the McCalls' home for the real estate section of the Sunday Springfield newspaper when my phone went off. It was Detective Harrington.

"I finally got through to Hascomb, and he contacted his client. Apparently, Miller has a nine o'clock class and can't come into the police station until eleven. I was tempted to go roust him out of his dorm and let his lawyer meet him here. But we still don't have any evidence directly connecting him to Teller's death. Even if the Fitzsimmons girl did go to see him, I doubt he would have killed her if he had nothing to do with Teller's death."

"It would still be good to know if he talked to her. She might have given him some hint about her source."

"I agree."

"Did you hear from Doctor McCall yet?"

"Teller's doctor. Why would he call me?"

I told him about last night's conversation with the McCalls.

"So you think Teller might have been incapacitated enough to be an easy victim, even for Rockwell Boyd?"

"The thought came to mind."

"You know it occurred to me that if you could get Boyd to handle something and then bring it back to us, we could get a set of his prints to match against what we found in Teller's office without having to go through all that procedural rigmarole."

"What did you have in mind?"

"We found a plaque that Teller received when he won a journalism award back in the day. We've checked it for prints already. Why don't we shine it up, then you can hand it to Boyd and ask if he's ever seen it before? Make sure he handles it. Then take it back and we'll lift his prints from it."

"It might be tricky to get him to touch it."

"Ask him to read it and tell you whether he's ever seen it before. Make up some story if you have to about how it may lead to the identity of the killer."

"I'll give it a try."

"Great. I'll have it ready for you when you come in at eleven. By the way, make sure you're carrying when you go to see Boyd this afternoon. You never know what might set him off if he is the killer."

I told him I would. After I hung up I spent the next few minutes finishing my ad on the McCall house for the newspaper. I called it in to the Springfield newspaper but decided to deliver it by hand to *The Sentinel*. It would give me a chance to talk with Myra and find out how to send in my stories by e-mail to the paper. In the back of my mind, I was probably also hoping to see Daniel again. There was a side of me that was unhappy with the way we had parted and was still hoping for a more satisfying conclusion. Another side of me said to walk away and forget about it.

I walked through the door of *The Sentinel* just as Myra hung up the phone.

"I was afraid that I was never going to see you

again," she whispered.

"I need to get some advice on how to send in my stories."

"No problem." She glanced down the hallway to where Daniel had his office. "He's been an absolute bear since the two of you broke up."

"He told you about that?"

"More or less. He came in and announced that from now on your relationship would be purely professional, then he marched down the hall to his office before I could even react. Was it because of Bianca?"

"Not just that," I said, not wanting to explain anymore.

She nodded. "It doesn't help when a man is too attached to his mother. Have you ever met her?"

"Once."

I recalled the one time I'd had dinner at Daniel's house, a dinner he'd prepared because his mother had claimed to be feeling under the weather that day. As we sat around the table, she'd gone on and on about what a good son Daniel was and how he did everything for her. She would frequently reach out to touch him on the arm as if physically asserting her rights. Daniel had sat there with a pained smile on his face and heroically tried to change the subject. But try as he might, she continually brought the conversation back to herself and her son. Clearly, she wanted me to know that whatever I might be to Daniel, it was weak and transitory compared to the mother and son bond. I'd sat there and struggled to smile politely, aware that if she'd had her way I'd be lying dead on the floor.

"Then you know how creepy she can be."

I nodded.

"You'd wish he'd stand up to her more, but of course, a boy can't just walk away from his mother."

"I guess not."

"At any rate, he's been as grumpy as can be since the two of you broke up. He takes my head off about the least little thing."

We heard Daniel's office door open and both of us looked behind us as we heard his footsteps coming down the hall. There was indeed a scowl on his face as he walked into the lobby.

"Where is the file—?"

He stopped and stared when he saw me.

"Kate," he said.

"I just stopped by to learn how to submit my stories," I explained quickly, not wanting him to think that I had come to see him.

"Let's go into my office," he said, turning on his heel and heading back up the hall.

Myra looked at me inquisitively. I shook my head, having no idea what Daniel wanted unless he planned to fire me before I'd even started as a reporter. I walked into his office, and he closed the door behind me then motioned that I should sit down in the chair across from his desk. Now I was certain I was about to be fired. He sat forward and leaned his elbows on the desk.

"Kate, I just wanted to apologize for the way I've acted toward you recently. This whole thing with Joe Teller's death and then Bianca's has cut me loose from my moorings, and I haven't been myself. I'm sorry I was such a jerk the other night at the restaurant, acting like there was no good reason in the world for you to break up with me. I realize that I'm no prize, what with my mother, my obsession with working at a poor paying job, and my recent blindness to Bianca. I'm surprised that you stayed with me as long as you did."

I felt more uncomfortable listening to Daniel list his faults than I had when he was listing mine. I had wanted us to have a conversation, but this was going in a way I didn't like. Confessions were often followed by attempts at reconciliation, and I wasn't looking for that.

"Look, Daniel, I don't think it's your fault or mine that we broke up. We were just at different points in life and not ready to get together for the long run."

He shook his head. "You're being generous. I'm more to blame, and I admit it."

"I don't think there's any point in assessing blame right now," I said, itching to get up and leave the room.

He ran a hand across his brow. "Of course, you're right. I'm handling this badly again. I just wanted to say that I'd like us to remain friends. I know I was abrupt on the phone with you yesterday, and I don't want that to be the tone of our working relationship."

"That's fine with me," I said, knowing I sounded a bit perfunctory.

"I realize that you can't commit to anything yet, but I don't want to lose you from my life."

"Don't worry I'll still be around," I said, struggling to sound lighthearted.

He walked around the desk and opened his arms. I stood up, ready to bolt.

"A friendly hug?" he asked.

Awkwardly I put my arms around him. His body felt familiar, but it seemed odd not to be able to relax into him. I pulled away quickly.

"Friends?" he asked.

"Of course," I said. Turning quickly I left the office.

Myra looked up at me as I entered the lobby.

"Do you want me to show you how to send a story?"

"I don't really have the time now." All I wanted to do was leave before Daniel made a more concerted pitch for us to get back together again, which I suspected was already on his mind.

"No problem," Myra said. She handed me a small pamphlet. "We give this out to all new reporters. I think everything you need to know is in there. If you have any questions give me a call." She paused and winked. "Calling might help to avoid any awkwardness."

I gave her a smile of thanks. "I'll do that," I said.

"But don't be a stranger. I'd like the chance to talk with you once in a while."

"Okay," I said, squeezing her arm and heading out the door. It felt good to be in the open air.

* * * *

Evan Martin sat across from me looking a bit paler than last time. Dark circles under his eyes indicated that he hadn't been sleeping well. Attorney Hascomb didn't look any happier than his client at being there. I figured it had been years since he'd spent this much time in a police station. His straitlaced ancestors probably wouldn't have approved.

"I told you last time that my client has nothing more to say about the alleged accusation of plagiarism."

"Fine, we're not interested in that today," Harrington said. "Today we'd like to talk about Bianca Fitzsimmons."

"Isn't that the young woman who died up at

Minton State?" asked the lawyer. "What could that possibly have to do with my client?"

"She was looking into Professor Teller's death, and she knew that Teller thought your client had committed plagiarism."

"Did Bianca come to see you?" I asked the boy before Hascomb could raise any objections.

He shook his head.

"C'mon," Harrington said impatiently. "She was into this story and would have wanted to talk to you right away."

"My roommate, Seth, said she came by to see me at the dorm, but I was staying with my cousin. I didn't see her."

"Did she tell Seth why she wanted to see you? Didn't he give you a call to say she'd come by?" I asked.

"She didn't say anything to Seth, and he didn't know how to reach me. I only found out she'd been there when I returned to my room the next day."

Where had Bianca gone next? If she couldn't talk to Evan, she had probably gone to her secret source to see if that person could tell her any more about the plagiarism charge.

"When did Professor Teller let you know that he suspected you had plagiarized that paper?" I asked.

"About a week ago. He asked me to come to his office after class. When I got there he closed the door and made a big deal out of telling me that he didn't think I could have written that story. I insisted that I had, but he wouldn't believe me. He said he was going to have an Internet search done to see if he could find the sources I had copied from. Once he had gathered enough evidence to be certain I had plagiarized, he was going to discuss it with Professor Franks to decide on the penalty. He said it could range from getting an "F" on the paper to being expelled from the course with a failing grade. That would have ruined everything. I'd never have gotten into a top-notch graduate school."

"If your story was genuine, why didn't you simply produce the student you had interviewed? That would have gotten Professor Teller off of your case," asked Harrington.

"I tried. He'd been sleeping on the floor in a friend's room in one of the dorms when I talked to him, but he disappeared a few days later. He left his friend a cell phone number. I called several times and left messages, but he never got back to me."

"What about this friend? He could at least verify that the guy was staying with him."

"I tried to get him to come with me to talk with Professor Teller, but he was afraid of being tossed out of the dorm for allowing an unauthorized person to stay there. He refused to have anything to do with it."

"It sounds to me like the police might want to pay this student a visit," Hascomb said.

"We'll look into it," Harrington responded. "What's his name?"

"Gregory Bishop," Evan said. Harrington wrote it down in his notebook.

"Did anyone else know that Teller was thinking of bringing charges against you?" I asked

Evan shook his head.

"You didn't tell any of your friends?"

"I didn't want it getting around the school."

"What about your parents?"

"God, no! They'd have been so upset they'd have wanted to sue the school and Professor Teller. Then everyone would know."

"Are they going to sue now?" I asked.

"I've convinced them to wait until the outcome of this inquiry," Attorney Hascomb said somberly.

"So no one other than the student you interviewed and the fellow he was staying with knew about the plagiarism matter?" I asked.

Evan nodded. "I didn't tell anyone else. I don't know who Professor Teller told."

Aside from Jessica Franks, the department chair, there was no one else that I knew Teller to have told, and he hadn't told even her the student's name. From what I knew of him, he didn't strike me as the kind of guy who would spread around uncorroborated accusations.

Harrington gave me an inquiring look to see if I had any more questions. I shook my head.

"That will be all for now, Mr. Miller," Harrington said. "Thank you for coming in."

"And I expect the police to look into my client's claim that he did not plagiarize this story. If he didn't, he would certainly have no motive for harming Professor Teller."

"We'll check it out," the detective said.

When Evan Miller and Hascomb had left the room, Harrington turned to me.

"What did you think of the kid's story?" he asked.

"It had enough detail to sound plausible. Plus he gave you a name you can check out. He wouldn't have done that if he was making it all up."

"That makes it sound more and more like Rockwell

Boyd is our man," Harrington said. He handed something in a plastic bag across the table to me. "This is the award I want Boyd to handle. Hold it by the wire on the back when you take it out of the bag, so you don't get your prints on it."

"I'll take care of it."

"When do you go see Boyd?"

"Two o'clock."

"Like I told you before, bring your gun, and better carry some cuffs."

"Okay," I said, smiling to myself as I tried to picture the trim, dapper professor becoming a violent physical threat. Then I warned myself not to misjudge him. If he had killed Teller, he didn't mind getting his hands dirty.

"In fact," Harrington went on, "I think I'll come along as backup. I'll wait outside in front of the building. I don't want him to see me; it might increase his suspicions."

"If it will make you feel better."

"It will. But you know what will make me feel really good? Catching this murderer before he kills again."

Chapter Thirty-Five

I trudged up the stairs of Dillard Hall hoping this was the last time I'd have to make the trip to the English Department. I'd spotted Detective Harrington sitting in his unmarked car across the way from the building and given him a discreet nod. I didn't think I'd need him, but it gave me a warm feeling to see him there all the same. I had my gun on my hip, my cuffs on my back, and was carrying the award plaque in my hand like I was on the way to make a presentation. I walked right past the Department office and down the hall to Boyd's. I was a few minutes early, so I walked farther down the hall to Teller's office, trying to imagine what it had been like that afternoon when Boyd made his way down there and pushed his colleague out the window—all for a job. Of course, I'd known people who had killed for less but usually it was in the heat of passion, when they were too angry, drunk, or frightened to realize what they were doing. If Harrington and I were right, Boyd had done this with calm deliberation. On a certain level, I still found it hard to believe that this scholarly man would kill someone just to keep his teaching job, but you don't have to be a cop for long to learn that people's motives often don't seem to justify their actions.

I walked back to Boyd's office. The door was still closed. It occurred to me that he might have arrived early and be sitting in there waiting for me to knock, so I rapped on the door. There was no response, so I tried the handle. The door opened. I took a couple of steps inside. He was sitting behind his desk, leaning back in the chair as if the to catch the sunlight coming in through the window.

"Professor Boyd…"

He didn't move. I took a couple more steps, the hairs on the back of my neck starting to rise. It wasn't until I was almost up to the desk when I saw the red blotches on the front of his denim shirt. His eyes were open, staring blankly across the room. He wouldn't be worried about keeping his job anymore. For a moment I stood frozen in shock then my training kicked in and I scanned the top of his desk for the knife he'd taken away from the mugger. I didn't see it. I heard the old wooden floor creak behind me and spun around, my heart pounding in my chest.

Fiona Halsey stood in the doorway, her mouth open wide. I thought she was going to scream, but instead she said, "What's happened?"

"Professor Boyd has had an accident," I said, remembering Janet Phillips advice to be gentle with the girl.

She didn't say anything, just stood there so tense she was almost vibrating.

"When did you see Professor Boyd last?" I asked to break her out of her trance.

"He came into the office this morning to get the code for the anti-plagiarism software."

I glanced at the desktop again and didn't see Evan Martin's paper. Whoever had killed Boyd had taken it; probably thinking it was the only copy.

251

"The paper has disappeared. Well, I guess Evan will be relieved to find out that he's off the hook," I said.

"I'm sure he will," she said with a sudden smile of triumph.

I gave her a searching look. "How did you know that it was Evan Martin's paper that was being checked?"

She frowned. "Professor Boyd must have told me."

"I don't think he would have revealed the name to another student."

"Maybe I heard Professor Teller say it to Professor Franks."

"No, he never told her the student's name." I paused for a moment. "What I think happened is that you heard him say to her that he was investigating a case of plagiarism and you saw him leave her office with a paper in his hand. Later, after Professor Teller left his office, I think you used the master key to enter his office and see whose paper it was."

Fiona's eyes went wide, and I knew that I'd made a lucky guess.

"I couldn't believe it was Evan's paper. I never thought he'd do anything like that," she said.

"Is Evan a friend of yours?"

"We've been in classes together. When he comes into the Department office, he always stops to talk with me. He's a nice guy."

"So you wanted to help him?"

She nodded and her face got the intense look of someone with an infatuation. "I should have taken the paper the first time I went into Professor Teller's office, but I was so surprised to see that it was Evan's, I left without doing anything. I had to think about it."

"And once you had time to think about it, you decided to return to his office and get the paper. But he caught you searching, didn't he?"

"Yes. I tried to tell him I was just putting some papers on his desk, but he saw me closing a desk drawer and went ballistic. He was going to drag me down the hall and report me to Professor Franks. I'd have been fired." Her eyes filled with tears. "This job is all I have. I couldn't let him do that."

"So you fought with him and pushed him out the window." I noticed again that she was almost as tall as myself when she stood up straight. Her shoulders were broad and her arms long.

"I didn't even know the window was open. He must have opened it earlier. We were pushing and shoving each other and went all the way across the room. I gave him one desperate last push, and before I realized he had toppled out the window. I didn't know what to do, so I ran. I didn't even bother to keep looking for the paper."

"But when Bianca came to you to find out what you knew about Professor Teller's death, you had to come up with a story that would protect Evan and yourself. So you told her about the dean and Professor Boyd."

She nodded with a shrewd glint in her eye. "I'd given Bianca information before. People talk in front of me; they forget that I'm even there."

"Were you Bianca's friend?"

"No," she almost shouted. "Bianca just wanted to use me to get gossip. She thought I was so pathetic that I'd tell her anything if she were only a little nice to me.

But I showed her."

"When you suffocated her?"

Fiona gave a small smile. "She thought I was coming to her room to give her some information on Evan. The little fool really thought I would betray Evan to her. She didn't even know I was the one who hit her on the head. She thought it was Evan. Bianca was too dangerous to live. Eventually, she'd have stumbled on the truth."

"And then Professor Boyd came to you today for the software to check Evan's paper, so you knew it wasn't over."

"I went to his office and begged him not to do it. I told him that it would destroy Evan's future. But he wouldn't listen to me. He said he had to do it or he would lose his job. So I picked the knife up off of his desk, and after it was over, I took the paper and ran it through the shredder." She smiled. "Evan is safe now."

"He was safe all along. I don't think Evan ever plagiarized that paper. You should have had more faith in your friend. He is a good person. So you've killed three people for no reason."

Her face became a mask of shock. "You mean I didn't protect him."

"He never needed it."

"So he won't appreciate that I did him a favor? He won't know that I did it all for him?"

"It's time you turned yourself in, Fiona. I'm sure people will understand why you did it."

Her face suddenly became firm and determined. "No, they won't. People never understand me."

Her right hand came out from behind her back holding the knife. I felt tightness in my gut as if I were already experiencing the pinch and the pain of the knife entering my body.

"Don't do anything foolish, Fiona, it's all over."

I mentally measured the distance between us, with one stride of her long legs, she would be within striking distance. If she was fast, I might not even have a chance to get the gun off my hip. She held the knife in close to her body with the blade in front of her. I could see her starting to come forward on her toes, ready to lunge. Suddenly I realized that I was still holding the plaque. I let it drop to have my shooting hand free. It clattered to the floor. Fiona glanced down in surprise, wondering what it was.

I had an idea. I bent down as if I were going to pick up the plaque. Instead, I grabbed the end of the Persian rug and gave it a powerful pull, putting my legs into it and backing up several feet. The rug moved easily on the polished floor, and Fiona went flying backward. She fell into the bookcase behind her, hitting her head with a thud. Momentarily stunned, she was already staggering to her feet as I leapt across the space between us. I kicked hard at her knife hand and saw the blade go flying into the corner across the room. I pushed her hard, knocking her to the floor then I came down with both knees in the center of her chest. The breath whooshed out of her body. Before she could recover, I flipped her over and cuffed her hands.

She was already struggling under me by the time I located my phone and called Harrington.

"Do you need help?" he asked.

"I definitely do," I said.

"I'll be right there."

I settled my knees onto Fiona's lower spine so she

wouldn't fight as much, relieved that help was close at hand.

Chapter Thirty-Six

The next two days passed in something of a daze. I knew what I was doing, but it seemed like someone else was going through the motions. I spent a lot of time in the police station explaining exactly what had happened. Harrington and I worked out a story where we made it sound like we had been much more organized than we really were and had at least suspected Fiona's involvement. I also played down my role in the apprehension, so it didn't appear as though my life had been at risk. We knew we had to do this so Harrington could avoid the wrath of the chief, who, from what I had heard, was already seething about my close involvement in the case.

When I wasn't at the police station, Daniel and I were working on a story to get into the Saturday edition that would detail—at least to the extent that we were allowed—the three murders and the apprehension of the killer. We didn't mention Evan Miller because his alibi panned out. The police talked to the student who had allowed the subject of the story to stay in his room, and he reluctantly confirmed Evan's claim. Again, we played down my part in the final takedown, although anyone reading between the lines would probably guess that my involvement was more than described. My dad was one of those who guessed because he called me at work that afternoon.

"I read the paper today." He stopped to chuckle. "It sounds like you're up to your old tricks again. Let me congratulate you on a job well done. Your mother, of course, is less than thrilled, but even Amanda seems rather impressed. In fact, she'd like to talk to you about it when you have time. I guess she wants to get some pointers for her future career."

"I have a date tonight and an open house tomorrow afternoon, but tell her Sunday night would be fine."

"You have a date tonight. Good. I'm glad to hear that you're getting right back into the game."

"It's not much of a game. At least I don't find it to be fun."

"I can dimly remember what it was like back before I met your mother. Men get nostalgic about that period of their lives when they reach middle age, but if they were honest with themselves, I doubt many of them actually enjoyed it all that much."

"But you have to keep looking."

"I guess that's true. You never know when you'll find the right one."

The date that night actually went better than I expected. Andrew may not be the right one, but he turned out to be a clever, funny guy who seemed to enjoy my sense of humor. He, too, had read the newspaper story on the Minton State Murders, as they were being called in papers across Massachusetts. I gave him a few facts that weren't in the story, but not enough to get Harrington or me into trouble. You never know whom a lawyer might meet, and I didn't know Andrew well enough to trust him to keep a confidence. He, in turn, told me a bunch of stories about what the law is like from the defense attorney's side, and I will admit that I came away with some sympathy for the job he has to do.

I asked enough questions to find out that he had a pretty successful practice for an attorney working in a small town and that his parents lived a safe distance away in Rhode Island. I wanted to make sure that at least I wouldn't be repeating the same mistakes I'd made with Daniel. I wanted a man who could afford to settle down and had no emotional ties preventing him from doing so. That wasn't enough for me to love a man, but it was enough to keep him on the list.

We ended the evening in the parking lot of the inn exchanging a sweet kiss that could have become more ardent if I hadn't been determined to take things slow. We left it that we would definitely be in touch during the week.

The next morning when I woke up, instead of being full of excitement over my date, I felt exhausted. I hadn't slept well, and it wasn't because visions of Andrew were dancing in my head. Fiona Halsey held that place. I kept seeing her expression, as she was poised, ready to come at me with that knife. The look of determination and absolute absence of fellow feeling was unnerving. It was the blank face of evil. I had added a new dream to my album of nightly horrors.

My morning run helped dissipate the images somewhat, as did a good long house cleaning. In the afternoon, I went down to the town green to see a show of local art. I was surprised by how many people I recognized, and how many mentioned seeing my name in *The Sentinel*. I tried to take comfort in the beautiful setting and being among people I knew, however casually. The ambience of a small town washed over me, and the tensions of the day slowly loosened. What I had done had been for these people, and I would continue to work for them in whatever role I took up in life.

I was looking at a painting of a vase of flowers when I became aware of someone standing next to me. It was the chief.

"I wasn't happy about your involvement in the Teller case," he said, staring straight ahead. "I know the report Harrington gave me was a bunch of crap, and you had a bigger part in all this than he let on."

He paused, and I waited to hear what threats would follow.

"But at least you and Rencardi didn't play up your role in *The Sentinel* article. You made it sound like the department did all of the work, so I guess it's all right. You did a good job. Let's just hope it doesn't happen again."

Not saying anymore, he nodded to the couple behind us and walked away. Probably feeling good, just as I did, about living in a town that he kept safe.

That evening after supper, I settled onto the sofa ready for a quiet evening of television, but my lack of sleep caught up with me and I dozed. A knocking on the door woke me up. I looked at the clock and saw that an hour had passed. Staring through the peephole, I saw Amanda mugging at me.

"How are you, sis?" she asked when I opened the door.

"Good," I said in a voice that sounded unconvincing even to me.

"That's what I thought. I figured I'd come by and we could go out for a stiff one. But then I remembered that I'm too young to drink. So how would you like to go out for an ice cream soda? We could talk about things that have been happening lately. Maybe you could even tell me about your date."

"I'll tell you about mine if you'll tell me about yours," I said.

The words had slipped out inadvertently, and I was afraid I'd offended Amanda. She blushed, but then a valiant smile came over her face.

"Who knows? Maybe I will. Maybe I just will."

A word about the author…

Glen Ebisch taught philosophy in college for over twenty-five years, and for the same period of time has been writing mysteries, first for young people, then for adults. He has been fortunate enough to have over twenty published. He lives with his wife in western Massachusetts and now focuses full time on writing, exercise, and travel.

http://www.glenebisch.com